DESOLATION - AN APOCALYPTIC NOVEL

KELLEE L. GREENE

From Below Series

Creatures - Book 1

Desolation - Book 2

Red Sky Series

Red Sky - Book 1

Blue Cloud - Book 2

Black Rain - Book 3

White Dust - Book 4

Indigo Ice - Book 5

Yellow Heat - Book 6

Ravaged Land Series

Ravaged Land -Book 1

Finding Home - Book 2

Crashing Down - Book 3

Running Away - Book 4

Escaping Fear - Book 5

Fighting Back - Book 6

Ravaged Land: Divided Series

The Last Disaster - Book 1

The Last Remnants - Book 2

The Last Struggle - Book 3

Falling Darkness Series

Unholy - Book 1

Uprising - Book 2

Hunted - Book 3

The Island Series

The Island - Book 1

The Fight - Book 2

The Escape - Book 3

The Erased - Book 4

The Alien Invasion Series

The Landing - Book 1

The Aftermath - Book 2

Destined Realms Series

Destined - Book 1

It had been about four days since I'd lost my mom to the creatures. I couldn't even remember how long it had been since they'd killed my dad. Even though Marty and I weren't alone, it was hard not to feel that way.

We were with our neighbors, Austin and Noah, whose parents had also been killed, and my ex, and his fiancé. The six of us had absolutely no idea what we were doing.

During the day, we'd try to find things we could use from inside the house but with the giant hole in our basement floor, no one dared to stay inside for too long. We didn't trust the flashlights and the sunlight to be enough to keep the creatures away. For all we knew, one day the creatures would decide to be brave enough to face the light.

The first day after they'd taken my mom, we could hear them below making their noises. They knew we were out there and they wanted more.

Austin had set up a light just above the hole but the house was such a disaster inside that it was difficult and unsafe to navigate most parts of the first floor. We could gather food and we'd been able to get some blankets but beyond that, it would have just been too dangerous.

There wasn't much we could do with the house but we didn't have anywhere to go. It would have been hard for me to leave it behind, not that I had told anyone that. It had been my home all my life and seeing it in its current condition was depressing.

I'd spent most of my life waiting for the day I could leave and be on my own but now, I didn't know how I could do it.

The generator kept the lights that Austin had rigged on the outside of the house glowing through the night but still we turned on the ones he'd set up on the vehicles as well. It wouldn't ever feel like there would be enough light. Someone was always awake during the night to keep watch but more often than not it was most of us. It was easier to sleep during the day.

The creatures didn't come close but we could still see them out there in the distance watching and waiting for an opportunity. They weren't going to give up. If we were all that was left, their last chance at food, they wouldn't just walk away.

During the day, I struggled to get much of any sleep thanks to the horrible nightmares that occurred every time I closed my eyes. If I wasn't reliving what had happened to my dad, I was reliving the loss of my mom. She'd always be pulled away from me and the sounds I'd heard when they captured her had been ingrained into my memory.

It was torture.

Hopefully, she hadn't suffered.

Hopefully, she was with my dad and they were looking down on us doing whatever they could to keep us safe. Our guardian angels and boy did we need them.

The creatures had come from the underground but we didn't have a clue what they were. They were some kind of new species that had evolved and managed to find their way through the surface. It was probably all we'd ever know since there wasn't anyone left to find out exactly what they were and tell us more about them.

What we'd learned so far was that it seemed as though the creatures were blind and used sonar to move about but still, they were terrifyingly powerful. Their long sharp claws could get through anything except for the light. The light would stop them quicker than a bullet although the bullets seemed to work just fine too.

Our situation felt hopeless but yet we didn't talk about it. At least not much. Hell, Marty barely even talked to me at all anymore. But none of us were ready to throw in the towel. None of us wanted the creatures to win.

"I think I'm going to head into town today," Austin announced during breakfast which wasn't anywhere near as good as what my mom would have prepared. All I'd been able to do was find a box of granola bars and pass them around to the others.

"Oh?" I asked feeling my heart clench at the idea of being away from him.

"I think we should find more weapons. The shotgun worked pretty good but still, we should have more," Austin said. "Something for each one of us. Plus, extra for good measure."

Noah's head was bobbing up and down in agreement. "Dad had lots of guns... maybe we can dig through the rubble and find some from back home."

"Hmm, that's a good idea," Austin said glancing in my direction. He could tell I was uneasy with the idea of them going into town. "And not as far away."

I swallowed down a hard lump and tried to force a smile. Surely it must have appeared to be something closer to a grimace based on the awkward pull of the muscles in my face.

"I don't know how to even use a gun." Mallory frowned.

"I'll teach you," Bradley said.

My head fell to the side and I stopped my eyes during mid-roll. "Do *you* know how to shoot a gun?"

"Well, sort of," Bradley said. "Surely I could hit one of those huge things."

"I'll teach them," Marty said.

Austin placed his hands on his hips and surveyed our surroundings. "I'm not sure how I feel about all the noise it'll make."

"Better to make some noise during the day than to not know how to shoot and be faced with one of those things during the night, right?" Marty asked with an excited grin. He knew he was right and it seemed to give him a noticeable thrill.

If it bothered Austin in any way, he didn't let it show. It wasn't that Austin had considered himself the leader of our little group, it just so happened to work out that way.

If anything happened to him, we'd be in serious trouble, not that I dared to say that out loud and jinx us. But I was pretty sure everyone in the group thought the same thing anyway.

"You ready?" Austin asked bumping Noah lightly with his elbow.

"Yep," Noah said without hesitation.

They were walking toward the truck before I even realized what was happening.

"So soon?" I asked grabbing Austin's arm and turning him to face me.

"The sooner we leave, the sooner we'll be back," he said with a shrug as he looked up at the pale blue morning sky.

The clouds were so fluffy it was hard to believe that anything less than perfect was happening around us. It was hard to believe how much had changed as I watched a cloud that looked like an elephant float by and turn into a rhinoceros.

"What should we do here?" I asked feeling my nerves twinge as I lowered my eyes back down to the devastation surrounding us. It would have been nice to look back down and realize it had all been a dream but that didn't happen. That wasn't going to happen.

"Stay here," Austin said gesturing toward the lawn chairs that had been positioned under one of the big lights. They were right next to the grill and the picnic table making it all look more like we were about to have a barbecue. "Don't look so worried."

My mouth dropped. "I am worried."

"We'll be back long before dark," Austin said. "If

we can't find anything at our place, we'll come right back." He placed a kiss on my forehead even though everyone was watching us. "If it makes you feel better, I won't go into town without you."

I swallowed so hard it made me wince. "This feels like it's too far, too soon."

"Got your phone?" he asked without giving me a chance to respond. "Don't answer that, I'll message Marty if I need to contact you."

"What happens when we can't charge our phones any longer?" I asked. It was a question I was mostly asking because I knew it would keep him next to me a little longer.

Austin grinned. "You can charge it in the SUV."

"What about when we can't use them at all," I asked.

"Then, we'll all stick together or maybe find some two-way radios," Austin said tapping his finger to his chin. "Dad might actually have some."

"Maybe we should all stick together now," I said biting my lip. With how clingy I was acting I should have just jumped onto his back and wrapped my arms and legs around him like a baby monkey.

That wasn't the kind of person I was. This world was turning me into something I wasn't and I wasn't all that happy about it.

Austin placed his hands on my shoulders and drew

in a calming breath. His eyes were focused on mine and I knew he wanted me to mimic his serenity.

"If you don't want me to go I won't," he said tilting his head slightly.

"Well," I said quickly glancing back at the others.

I wasn't ready to leave Marty yet either, although, I'd be more than happy to leave Mallory and Bradley behind. Marty was listening and shifting his weight nervously even though he was pretending to be looking at something quite interesting on the ground near his feet.

"Just go fast," I whispered before biting my cheek to stop myself from saying anything more.

"We will," Austin said giving my shoulders a brief squeeze. "I promise."

He turned away and I couldn't help but wonder if it would be the last time I'd see him. I probably should have dropped to my knees and begged him to take us all with him... but I didn't. There was still some of me left inside which was hopefully a good thing.

I had to trust that he wouldn't do something he knew would be dangerous. Even though it was hard, I had to believe he wouldn't leave if he thought for a second that something would go wrong.

But that was the problem with our new world. We didn't know if or when something would go wrong.

There wasn't anything safe. Anything could go

wrong at any moment, although, with the sun above and more than enough gas for the generator, our chances felt a little bit better. At least, for the time being.

The truck started and the rumbling engine noises vibrated through my stomach. As Austin drove away from the house, it felt like the small pieces of my heart that remained, were being pulled apart like taffy being stretched to its breaking point.

Once I couldn't see the truck any longer, I turned around to face the others. They were looking at me as if they needed to be told what to do.

An idea struck me. It was the perfect time.

I cocked my head to the side and grinned like the Grinch on Christmas Eve. "I have an idea."

CHAPTER TWO

Marty's eyes widened. "Now, I'm worried."

I ignored him.

"So," I said pointing out at the field where I'd spotted one of the holes. "Here's what we're going to do."

"You're going to put us to work?" Mallory said as if she could sense some sort of shift in the atmospheric pressure that warned her that she might have to actually do something physical.

I cocked my head to the side. "Yeah, sort of anyway."

"It's kind of warm," Mallory groaned as she fanned herself dramatically. "I don't really want to sweat when there isn't anywhere we can take a shower."

I ignored her. If I kept ignoring people, I was going to end up talking to myself.

"There's a hole in the ground over in that field. We're going to grab as much debris as we can from the barn and drop it down into the hole," I said.

"Why are we going to do that?" Bradley asked. "It's not like that's going to stop them. If it would have, it wouldn't be laying in a pile in the first place."

I shook my head and pointed my finger at him as if I were impressed. Finally, some common sense from Bradley. "No, no it probably won't stop them, but maybe it'll slow them. Think of it as an experiment."

"Why not pack the hole under the house?" Marty asked.

"We could but then I wouldn't be able to see what happens. Besides, that makes me nervous. There are just too many shadows in the house even with the light on," I said feeling a cool breeze that Mallory must have been immune to. "I just want to test it out. Tonight, maybe we'll hear them digging through all the debris and we can see how long it takes them to get through it all."

Marty gazed out at the field. After a long moment, he crossed his arms in front of his chest. "Okay, let's do it."

"I'll help," Bradley said rolling up the sleeves of his designer shirt. He caught me staring at him and smiled. "I can get a new one in town and at a very affordable price."

I raised my brow and decided it would be best to ignore him too. Three out of three on the ignore list. Of course, I knew it was impossible to ignore any of them but it made me feel better to think that I was.

"You should wait here," Bradley said as Mallory stepped up next to him and wrapped her hands around his arm. Cling wrap. When it came to Austin and me, I didn't want to be cling wrap. "Keep an eye out for Austin and Noah."

"Ooh! Yeah! I can totally do that," Mallory said releasing Bradley and plopping down in one of the lawn chairs so heavily it squeaked. She leaned back and crossed her long spidery legs as if she were impatiently waiting for a parade to start.

The three of us walked over to the barn. We stopped almost simultaneously and stared at the pieces of wood, metal, and the poor baby pig that was rotting beneath it all.

"Can't believe this was all your barn once upon a time," Bradley said. "I remember it so well."

My eyes shifted upward and rolled to the side. "It was just a barn."

"I know but it's just weird isn't it?" Bradley asked as he shook his head. "Such a shame."

I cleared my throat. "Over here."

They followed me to another pile of debris even

though they had probably already seen or at the very least smelled the poor thing.

I reached down and picked up a thick piece of wood that looked as though it had been snapped in two. One end was smooth and the other was rough and jagged. If I would have picked it up at the wrong end, I would have gotten several slivers.

"Careful with what you pick up. Could be some very sharp stuff here," I warned.

I carried a board in each hand, dragging the longer one behind me as I made my way down the driveway toward the field. Bradley was at my heels carrying an armful of wood.

As we got to the road, he caught up to me and looked both ways before crossing which had been unnecessary.

"So, Austin, he's your boyfriend, then?" he asked.

I hesitated and instantly wished I wouldn't have. It was just that we hadn't really talked about anything like that. Do I call him my boyfriend? It just seemed so weird... so unnecessary.

Bradley chuckled. "Are you embarrassed by him or something?"

"What? No," I said feeling the tension in my brow.

"Well, you know, I'm here. That has to be bringing back all kinds of feelings," Bradley said without looking at me.

I turned sharply and stared into his eyes. The amount of disgust that bubbled up inside of me like a pot about to boil over surprised me.

"You being here has nothing to do with anything. You and your fiancé barged in and made yourselves comfortable in my family's home," I said so sharply he jerked back ever so slightly. "We didn't invite you to stay."

"Your mom said it was okay," Bradley said defensively before pulling back his shoulders and tensing his jaw. I knew he didn't like to feel unwelcome. He thought everyone loved him and everyone always wanted to be by him. "If you wanted us to leave, you could have kicked us out at any time." He summoned his inner tough guy and leaned forward. "But you didn't."

Marty cleared his throat as he approached. It seemed as though he could feel the lack of oxygen in the area surrounding Bradley and me. That was something Bradley had a way of doing... sucking the life out of things.

"Where should I put this stuff?" Marty asked looking anxious to get away.

"Let's make a pile here," I said pointing near my feet as I kept my eyes glued to Bradley's. I wasn't finished with him but I needed Marty to leave before I could continue. "Go get more."

"So, I'm the only one that's going to do any actual work?" Marty asked.

My chest rose with anger. "Please?"

"Yes, boss," Marty said and I swallowed down my growl. It wasn't like I was mad at Marty but it was hard to stop the anger from radiating outward to anyone who stepped within a ten-foot radius.

After Marty walked back across the road, I chucked my smaller piece of wood onto the small pile.

"No one kicked you out because we don't want your blood on our hands," I said trying to regain my composure.

"Sounds to me like you still care what happens to me then," Bradley said with a smirk.

"No," I said throwing my hands into the air.

He squinted at me as if the sun had suddenly become too bright for his eyes. "Are you sure about that?"

"I'm positive. Beyond positive," I said confidently.

"I still care about you," Bradley said stepping around me to drop his pieces of wood onto the pile.

I let the bigger piece of wood drop heavily from my hand. "Bradley," I said with a soft chuckle, "you've never cared about anyone but yourself."

"That isn't true. I made a mistake. I knew you wouldn't ever understand, so I just left. Yeah, I'm a coward for that. I shouldn't have ever hurt you like I did," Bradley said. "It was a stupid mistake. I'll never forgive myself."

I snorted as I pointed across the road. "Fiancé. A fiancé," I repeated the word as if it were a punchline to a joke he wasn't getting. "Stop talking like that to me. You don't get to do that when you have a fiancé."

"Why? Is it bringing up unresolved feelings you have for me?" Bradley asked taking a step closer to me. His confidence was oozing out of his pores and dripping onto the ground. It made me want to vomit.

"I have absolutely no unresolved feelings for you whatsoever. Trust me, I've resolved them," I said crossing my arms as if that would somehow keep him from coming any closer. "Honestly, I have no idea why you're doing this. Why now? I have no interest in you. None."

Bradley chuckled. "I don't believe that. Not even for a second. I don't forget that easily. We were good together."

It felt like hundreds of creepy crawly bugs were under my shirt crawling all over my skin.

"Well, believe it." I exhaled slowly. "I didn't know it at the time but you and I had been a mistake since day one. There wasn't anything that good about it."

He shook his head wearing a sideways grin. "I just don't get it. Austin? I don't see it. He's not your type."

"Why does everyone keep saying that?" I muttered to myself. "I don't have a type."

Bradley took another step toward me and this time he was way too close. I took a large step back and held up my hand.

"Yes, he's my boyfriend," I said heat instantly filling my cheeks. I didn't care. "Now, kindly back off."

"Am I making you nervous?"

"No, you're creeping me out," I said.

"Okay, okay," he said holding up both palms. "You'll see, though."

I didn't want to ask what I'd see. All I wanted was to get more debris and fill the hole so we could get back to Mallory. The sooner we were back to her, the sooner he'd stop looking at me as if I were a popsicle on a hot summer day.

We started to walk back toward the barn. I kept my distance behind him but he turned and looked at me as he walked backward.

"You'll see you're making a mistake and when you do, I'll be there with open arms welcoming you back," Bradley said.

And the three of us would live happily ever after. Of course, I didn't want to actually say that out loud because he'd probably take me seriously.

I couldn't help but look at Mallory as I walked by. She was so completely oblivious and innocent. There was a part of me that wanted to walk over to her and tell her what had just happened.

She smiled at me before closing her eyes and stretching her limbs out as if she were trying to get a tan. A bigger part of me just wanted to keep the peace. There was no reason to upset her. She was alone. Bradley was all she had.

If I told her, it would be a big dramatic scene that I didn't want to be a part of. We had enough to worry about and there was no reason to create more.

I wasn't even sure if I should bother to tell Austin. It would just piss him off and really there was no reason to upset him either. I wasn't interested in Bradley and hopefully, he'd gotten that message.

After we hauled over a bunch of wood, we stood there nervously staring down the hole. There weren't any noises coming from below and there weren't glowing eyes staring back up at us.

"Now what?" Marty asked.

"Now, we start dropping it down there," I said picking up the sharp long piece I'd dragged over.

I let the long piece fall hoping it would impale one of the creatures on the way down. It took longer than I had expected for it to hit the bottom. The thud was soft by the time it had bounced back up to my ears.

We dropped pieces in one after the other until the hole was nearly filled.

"Guess we should have collected more," Marty said.

"Hmm, yeah. It's deeper than I thought," I said with my hands on my hips.

Based on the suns position, it was sometime just after noon. None of us had gotten much sleep and Mallory was frequently looking over at us. There was so much anxiety and boredom on her face that I could see it even at our distance.

"Finish tomorrow?" Bradley asked.

"Yeah, sure," I said even though it would probably be cleared out by morning.

All three of us looked up as Austin's truck barreled down the road as if he were competing in a race.

"Oh-oh," Bradley said with a smirk. "You're going to be in trouble."

I wanted to tell him he was an idiot, but I couldn't. He was probably right. Austin wasn't going to be thrilled that we were hanging out at the hole.

CHAPTER THREE

Austin slowed his truck and pulled into the driveway. He wasn't looking in our direction but I knew he'd seen us.

Both Austin and Noah hopped out of the pickup truck, walked to the back, and lowered the tailgate. They both stood there staring at whatever they'd collected.

I jogged ahead of Marty and Bradley and slowed my pace when I approached. Austin looked at me. There was a dark shadow from the brim of his hat that darkened his already dark eyes.

"We were filling the hole," I said as if I were compelled to explain.

"I figured," Austin said.

"Are you mad?" I asked keeping my voice low.

There was a pause that had felt like it had taken an

eternity. "No. I wish you would have waited for me, though."

"You left on your adventure," I said with a grimace.

"The hole is dangerous," Austin said.

My stomach sank lower. He was mad even though he probably wouldn't admit it.

"Heading out is dangerous, too," I said weakly.

He turned slowly but he stopped before his eyes had a chance to connect with mine.

"This is what we found," he said raising his voice as everyone gathered around the back of the truck.

My shoulders sagged. Maybe I should have waited for him. It wasn't like I had meant to do something that would piss him off. I'd only wanted to do something instead of sitting around and worrying.

"Wow," Bradley said reaching into the bed of the truck and pulling out a gun longer than his arm. "What's this?"

"A sniper rifle," Noah said.

"Why did your dad have a sniper rifle?" I asked.

Noah shrugged. "Just part of his collection. Might be fun to play with while wearing the night vision goggles."

Austin shook his head. "We brought it because it wasn't doing any good back at the house. Might as well bring what we could find here."

"I like this one," Mallory said picking up the

smallest one. She held it between her thumb and index finger as if the gun were long strands of hair she'd pulled out of a drain.

Austin gingerly took the gun from her and set it back down on the bed of the truck. "Let's just leave them all here for now... until we've all had some training."

Mallory shrugged before grabbing Bradley's bicep. She rested her head on his shoulder lovingly.

Bradley's eyes moved. He flashed me a satisfied grin when his eyes locked with mine. He couldn't have been more thrilled at having caught me watching them.

I rolled my eyes and looked away from him, turning back to Austin. He closed the tailgate and brushed his hands on his pants. Dust billowed up around him.

"Did you crawl around in the dirt?" I asked as we walked over to the SUV and away from the others. He was probably gearing up for his afternoon nap... the only time he slept and it never was for long.

"A little," he said. "Found a change of clothes too."

"Oh," I said noticing he hadn't changed into them. My eyes darted up to the second story of the house wishing I could go into my room and get myself a change of my own clothing.

He followed my gaze. "We can find stuff in town."

"Yeah, I know," I said fighting off the sadness I felt at having lost all of my things.

It wasn't like I had anything that I'd been particularly attached too but that hadn't meant I liked that it was all inaccessible. Losing my mom and dad was far worse than losing my things... they were just things and for the most part, they were all useless now.

"What are we going to do?" I asked clutching my mom's wedding ring that I kept tied to a piece of string around my neck. "Are we going to stay here forever?"

"I don't know," Austin said. "What do you think we should do?"

"You're asking me to decide?"

Austin scratched the back of his neck. "Why not? This is your home."

I glanced at Marty. He looked like he was about to fall asleep in one of the lawn chairs as Mallory blabbed on and on about something related to her fingernails.

"It's not just my decision. I want to do whatever is the safest and smartest thing to do," I said.

Austin nodded. "That might be staying here with the lights." He turned and stared at the field where we'd found the hole. "Or that might be leaving."

"Helpful," I teased with wide eyes.

"We could take a vote," Austin suggested.

My forehead wrinkled. "We could but that gives both Bradley and Mallory a say in our future and I'm not sure I'm comfortable with that."

I made sure I didn't look in Bradley's direction. It

was bad enough that what he'd said to me had still been fresh in my mind. Truthfully, I was feeling a bit angry with myself for not telling Austin about it but his eyelids were drooping lower and lower. I knew he needed his rest.

If I told him what had happened, he'd most certainly overreact. And it wasn't like I needed Austin to protect me from Bradley. I could take care of him all by myself.

"Think about it and we'll talk about it later," Austin said with an enormous yawn.

"I'm not exactly sure what to think about," I mumbled and Austin gave me a quick squeeze.

"I need to lay down before I fall down," he said.

I cocked my head to the side. "Do I need to worry about you?"

"Only if people die from a lack of sleep," Austin said and I narrowed my eyes at him. "I don't think they do. I haven't even started hallucinating yet. Unless you're not here."

Austin reached out and touched my head with both hands as if trying to decide if I were real or not. He thought he was hilarious.

I scrunched up my face at him and he chuckled.

"Stop wearing that face," he said lightly bumping his elbow into me.

"It's my 'you're not very funny' face," I said and he laughed harder.

"Okay, okay," he said holding up his palms. "I'll stop trying to be funny. Especially, when I'm this tired."

The small smile that had curled the sides of my lips vanished the instant I noticed Bradley watching us. I rolled my eyes and sighed a bit too loudly.

"Hey," Austin said looking into my eyes. My insides were like melted butter when my eyes connected with his soft, dark chocolate eyes. "I'm just teasing you. Everything is fine. I'm not even that tired."

"No," I said shaking my head and forcing a smile back onto my face. "It's not you. I guess maybe I'm tired, too."

"Maybe we should both take a rest in the SUV then," Austin said.

I shook my head even though the idea was tempting. The others might get ideas about what was going on and the idea of them all thinking that we were... no, it was perfect.

Austin shrugged and turned away from me but I grabbed his hand before he was able to get inside the SUV. He looked like he was fighting off another yawn.

"I changed my mind. Just let me tell Marty he's in charge," I said.

"You don't need to," Austin said dragging me along.

"Noah's staying up for a few hours. He'll keep an eye on things."

I wanted to turn and see if Bradley was still watching us make our way inside the van hand in hand but I also didn't want him to know that I would check first. He'd just twist everything so it would seem like the reason I'd been looking at him was because I was wishing it was him climbing into the SUV with me instead of Austin and I most definitely did not wish that.

Bradley was a thorn in my side. It was small but painful and there wasn't anything I could do to get the annoying thing out.

We'd only just made it inside the SUV as Mallory let out a scream that shot through the air like a fighter jet. I turned sharply expecting to see a creature clawing at her throat but there wasn't anything there. It was just Mallory standing there with her hands balled up at her sides shrieking for help.

Marty was down on his knees looking at something. As I blinked away my tiredness, I saw someone lying flat on the ground.

CHAPTER FOUR

Mallory stepped up to me with her mouth hanging open like she was about to let out another horrifying scream. But nothing came out of her mouth.

"What happened?" Austin asked kneeling down next to Marty.

"He just collapsed," Marty said shaking his head. "He was standing there and then all of a sudden he was on the ground. I think he's breathing."

I lowered myself to Bradley's other side and held his wrist lightly. It was hard to feel a pulse but only because Mallory's rhythmic whimpers were covering each beat.

"His pulse seems perfectly normal," I said shaking my head.

"Why would he just fall like that then? And why

won't he wake up?" Mallory asked. "Is he going to die?"

I shook my head. "He's not going to die."

"How do you know?" Mallory said before muttering something that sounded a lot like her stating that I wouldn't even care if he did. What had he said to her about me?

"Bradley," Austin said lightly rocking his body back and forth.

Bradley didn't open his eyes. Marty tapped his palm on Bradley's cheek. "Hey, man. Wake up, okay?"

"Get him some water," Austin said over his shoulder to Noah who was standing there watching from a short distance.

Noah appeared in a few seconds handing the bottle of water to Austin. Austin glanced at me and I wasn't sure if he was considering splashing him with it or if he was going to attempt to get him to take a drink.

Something took over and I reached over and grabbed the bottle from him. I hastily unscrewed the cap and poured the water on his face. I didn't have to look around to know that everyone had their eyes on me.

Bradley sat up abruptly. "Wh—what the hell?"

"See, he's fine," I said screwing the cap back on so tightly I didn't think anyone would be able to get it off again. I set it down next to him and got back to my feet.

Mallory stared at me wearing a look that was something between anger and thankfulness. She'd wanted to be mad at me but with having just brought Bradley back to life she didn't have any desire to care what I'd done to save him.

"What happened?" Marty asked Bradley as I made my way back toward the SUV.

"I'm not sure," Bradley said speaking louder than necessary. He wanted to make sure I could hear him. "Maybe I didn't eat enough today. I've been careful to eat only a little to make sure everyone else has enough."

Liar. Maybe the others wouldn't see through him, but to me, he was clearer than the windows of my fallen apart house. I wasn't going to be fooled by Bradley again. No way. No how.

I climbed into the SUV and made myself comfortable in the back. Austin had put the seats down to make more room and with the windows cracked it didn't get too hot or stuffy inside.

Clearing my mind was nearly impossible. I could still smell the sweet flowery perfume my mom used to wear as if it had permeated the fabric and flooring.

I hated being in the SUV alone. The truth was, I hated being alone at all because my mind would fill with the thoughts of what had happened to my parents.

There didn't seem to be anything I could do to

shake the images out. They'd play over and over again until I either eventually fell asleep or they'd stop when Austin laid down next to me.

Maybe we needed to get away from the house. Maybe we needed to find out if there was help out there.

The car door opened and Austin climbed inside the SUV. He laid down next to me and wrapped his arm around my waist.

The images disappeared.

"What was that all about?" Austin asked.

"What was what all about?" I asked deciding to play dumb even though I knew it wasn't going to work.

Austin propped himself up on his elbow and stared at me as if he were trying to dig deep inside my eyes to find answers.

"I'm not sure about that whole throwing water at him thing," Austin said with a shrug. "I mean, yeah, he's an idiot but—"

"He's a liar and a cheater and I'm sick of him being here," I blurted.

Austin looked stunned by what I'd said. It looked like he was letting my words sink in while he tried to find an appropriate response.

"Yes, he cheated on me," I said so he didn't have to ask about it. I was helping him process what I'd said a little faster. "And before you think otherwise, I don't care about it. I don't care about any of it. It's just awkward and stressful having him here. That's all."

He continued to stare. He was still searching for words.

"I really don't. I mean, obviously, it sucks to have been cheated on but if you think I still have feelings or not closure or whatever it is you're thinking, that's just not the case. It's just that I'm embarrassed I was with someone like that and he sort of disgusts me," I said with a firm nod. "Why would I want him here? Why do we have to take care of someone like that? And his fiancé too."

"We don't have to," Austin said finally finding his words.

I sighed. "If we don't, they'll die. They won't make it more than a day out there on their own."

"You don't know that," Austin said.

"I don't know but I'd bet our last light on it," I said trying to push away my frustrations. Devoting any amount of mental energy on Bradley was not only draining but it was also just infuriating. He didn't deserve my energy.

It made me feel sick that I was angry at Bradley. Not just for what he'd done today but for everything he'd done. It was like I wanted him to be punished. He didn't deserve everything he had. The life he'd had before. Most of all, I was mad that I was feeling anything because when it came to Bradley, I didn't want to feel anything. If I did, he was winning and that just made everything worse.

After everything I'd just said and how I'd reacted, I could tell that Austin was conflicted. He didn't know what to do or say to fix things. And that was where his mind had gone... he wanted to figure out a way to fix things for me.

There was no way I could tell him what Bradley had said to me in the field. Austin would kick him out not caring what time of day it was.

"I'm just so tired," I groaned and Austin pulled me closer.

"We all are. We are all on edge because of exhaustion," he said in a velvety tone.

I pressed my forehead to his chest. "I'll talk to him about it later. I guess I probably shouldn't have done that."

"You don't need to do that," Austin said. "He deserves to be splashed with a little water. Maybe it'll wake him up and he'll realize what he's lost."

"I don't want him to realize that," I said digging my fingertips into Austin. "All I want is you."

"You've got me," Austin said. "I think what you did was actually quite tame. He deserves something a bit harsher. Perhaps I should go out there and pour the rest of the water on him."

I smiled and looked up into his eyes. "It means a lot to me that you'd do that for me, but please don't."

"Are you sure? I'll do it if you want me to." Austin slowly pretended to get up. He almost seemed eager.

I held him closer. "I don't want that. Just stay with me while I sleep. That's what I want."

Austin brushed my hair back away from my face, tucking it behind my ear. He placed a soft, silky kiss on my lips.

"That what I want too," Austin said before resting his head on the pillow. He closed his eyes and the muscles in his face instantly relaxed. "But if he ever does anything that pisses me off, I won't hesitate to send him on his merry way."

It didn't take long for Austin to fall asleep. After a few minutes of silence, he was out.

CHAPTER FIVE

It was night but the surrounding area was brighter than a football field on Friday night. Austin, Noah, and Marty all held their guns as we stood near the SUV.

My eyes were focused on the field even though I couldn't see anything beyond the driveway. It was like the light hit a wall and it couldn't reach beyond a certain range.

Everyone was absolutely silent as we listened, waiting for the creatures to burst through the debris we'd stuffed inside their hole.

There were no noises coming from the hole across the road or from under the house. The only thing we could hear was the occasional sounds of the crickets

I didn't think for even a second that they were gone. They'd probably found something else to feast on temporarily.

"Lucy and I were talking," Austin said looking down at the gun in his hands. Everyone looked up at him. The volume of his voice had probably startled them more than the words he'd said. "We were thinking it might be time to head out and see what's out there.

My mouth started to drop but I quickly stiffened it so no one would notice. I wished Austin and I would have talked about it more although there wasn't anything that would change that would sway me one way or another.

"What if there isn't anything out there?" Marty asked flipping his phone around in his hand.

"We could always just come back," Austin said with a shrug.

"It might not be that easy," I said.

Austin turned to me with one brow raised. I shrugged.

"Well, we could have trouble finding gas," I said twisting my finger. "Or maybe we wouldn't even make it through the first night."

"The lights on the cars have been pretty thoroughly tested. I could get a backup battery just in case," Austin said crossing his arms. "I think we'd be pretty safe."

I stuffed my hands into my pockets so I didn't

throw them in the air. "A million things could go wrong."

"A million things could go wrong here," Austin said.

The other's heads shifted side to side as if they were watching a tennis match. It was the exact reason Austin and I should have discussed things privately and more thoroughly first.

I shook my head but not at his words. It was that I somehow thought that Austin needed to run things by me. I wasn't in charge. My only job in this group was to take care of Marty.

Anyone that wanted to leave could leave and anyone that wanted to stay could stay. I wasn't holding anyone at gunpoint.

Maybe Austin had been right about taking a vote. I hated the fact that Bradley and Mallory would each get one.

"We make a list," Austin said scanning each of our faces. He stopped on mine. "I wish I knew what was best for all of us but I don't. If we go, maybe we can find help."

"If we stay, maybe help will find us," I said.

Austin nodded. "It's possible. It's also possible there isn't help out there."

I studied Marty, trying to determine which way he

was leaning but he seemed preoccupied. It was almost as if he wasn't paying attention.

Marty turned on his phone. The glow wasn't even noticeable in the bright lights. He held it up, mostly in Austin's direction.

"I saw this," Marty said.

I took a step closer. It was a website with an address and the words 'We Save' in a large font across the top.

"Is there any way to know when that was posted?" Austin asked.

"It says it was updated yesterday," Marty said. "But there is no way of knowing if that's accurate."

"No way other than going there," Noah said.

Austin held out his hand. "Let me take a look."

Marty handed him the phone but there wasn't anything to see. There was no more information.

"Why wouldn't they post more?" Mallory asked her eyes dancing around as if she were worried ghosts were lurking over her head.

"This could be old," Austin said handing Marty the phone back.

Marty shrugged. "Could be but maybe it's not."

"What's the website address?" I asked.

Marty squinted at the screen. "The name of a church."

Austin and I exchanged a glance. It would take a day or two for us to pack up and several more days to drive there.

"What do we do if we get there and there isn't any help?" I asked.

"We could come back," Austin said with a shrug. "Or we could keep looking." He turned to Marty. "How did you find that website?"

Marty lowered his head. "I don't even remember... a rabbit hole of sorts."

"What do you think, Marty?" I asked.

"I'm not sure," he said refusing to meet my gaze. "What do you think?"

I glanced at the house as if the answer would suddenly appear on the outside walls. The weight of the decision wasn't something I wanted on my shoulders... it seemed as though no one did.

Austin might know the best ways to take care of everyone and to keep us safe but he was apparently a terrible decision maker. And the last thing I wanted was for Bradley or Mallory to weigh in.

I drew in a long breath. My chest deflated as I let it out.

"Okay, let's do it," I said.

"Yeah?" Austin asked.

"Are you sure?" Marty said at nearly the same time.

I scowled. "Don't make me second guess myself. Worst-case scenario we end up back here."

"That's not the worst-case scenario," Bradley said.

I turned to face him. "Anyone that wants to stay here can."

"Bradley," Mallory whined as she tugged on his arm.

Bradley cleared his throat. "We need a little privacy to discuss things. Mind if we use your car?"

"Go right ahead," I said gesturing toward the old beater.

They walked off hand in hand. Bradley opened the passenger side door for her before walking around to the other side. It was weird seeing him get into my car again but the further away from me he was the more oxygen we all had to breathe.

Austin and Noah went off, of course, not that far off, to work on a list of things they'd need to pick up either from their house or from town. I heard their soft words... it was going to just be the essentials, anything else we could find along the way. They didn't think it would be hard considering there wasn't anyone left to compete with for the remaining supplies.

They were going to put gas in the back of the SUV and in the back of his truck. We were going to take two vehicles. Austin would drive one and Noah would drive the other. More was better or so they thought because it would be more lights.

In town, they'd find food, car batteries, more ammunition, and they had plans to get big jugs of water from the grocery store. They sounded confident. They sounded almost excited.

"I hope this is the right thing to do," I muttered loud enough for just Marty to hear.

"I hope so, too," Marty said. "But I don't think help is coming for us. It's just that if any real help were out there, it would be on a real website. They'd be trying to contact people. Hell," Marty said throwing a hand toward the dark sky powdered with twinkling stars, "we'd probably hear planes, helicopters, or something, right?"

He was probably right but I couldn't even guess as to what should have been happening if there was help out there. Maybe there'd be explosions or gunfire as the army worked to thin the number of creatures. But there wasn't anything except for the sounds of the generator and us moving about.

Austin and Noah stepped up next to Marty. Austin had a list of words written on the back of his hand.

"New plan," he said grinning at me.

"Oh?" I asked almost afraid to hear what he was about to say.

His head bobbed and his eyebrows wiggled. "We'll leave in the morning, all of us. We can go into town together."

CHAPTER SIX

I sat on the step of the front porch letting the warm morning sun fill my body. The nights were cold and I needed to absorb as much sunlight as I could before we hit the road.

Austin and Noah were resting, preparing for our journey. There were about twenty minutes left before I would have to wake them and we'd be on our way.

They'd packed as much as they could during the night and we'd finish after they woke. I was feeling... weird. It felt like there was a hurricane in my stomach and it bubbled a sourness up into the back of my throat that put me on the verge of throwing up.

All my life, I'd dreamed of the day I'd leave home and be on my own but I never thought it would be like this. At least, I wouldn't be on my own.

I felt awful for all the times I'd wanted to get away

because now I'd do anything to have my parents back and be stuck in my home forever... if things would only go back to how they were. My life wasn't ever going to be the same.

We were about to head out to find other survivors... people we didn't know anything about. It was like I was feeling homesick and I hadn't even left home yet.

"Having second thoughts?" Marty asked squinting down at me. I wondered if he was tasting the same sourness I was.

"Not really," I said leaning back slightly to look into his eyes. If I looked deeply enough, maybe I could see how he truly felt. "It just feels weird to leave our home behind, I guess. Are you having second thoughts?"

Marty shook his head. "This doesn't really feel like our home anymore, at least not to me."

"Doesn't look like our home," I said my insides filling with sadness.

"Guess we're homeless," Marty said.

"Guess so," I said giving him a strange smile. "At least we're still together."

Marty nodded. The forlorn expression he wore was something that had been there since the moment our mom was pulled away from him.

"I wish there was something I could have done," I said and Marty paled before turning away from me.

It was like a big flashing neon sign appeared over his head indicating that losing our mom was something he didn't want to talk about. To be totally honest, I was just glad he was talking to me.

I cleared my throat hoping that he'd realized I received the message loud and clear. Maybe it wasn't something we could ever talk about.

I shakily got to my feet realizing that I needed to get something to eat. "It's time to wake them."

"Oh," Marty said moving his feet as if he couldn't get away from me fast enough. "I'll go get them."

My eyes widened briefly before shrinking back to their normal size. He was gone before I even had a chance to say another word.

I walked over to the stack of boxed-up bars next to one of the lawn chairs and popped open the box. It didn't even matter which flavor I had because I was just that hungry.

I devoured two bars before dropping the box back to the ground. Bradley was standing directly behind me as I turned.

"Jesus!" I said with a cough. A small piece of granola had gotten lodged at the side of my throat.

"So, sorry," he said placing his hand on my shoulder.

My eyes slowly moved down. It was like I almost expected to see snakeskin covering his arm.

"I didn't mean to startle you," Bradley said slithering around to my side. "It's just that I know how hard it is to leave your home behind."

Austin and Noah were climbing out of the back of the SUV. Austin shot a quick glance in our direction but he gave no reaction to Bradley standing so close to me.

He put his arm around my shoulder and a smile coiled onto his lips. The smile had been for Austin because when he turned back to me, it vanished.

"I know you don't give a shit but I lost my family and I had to leave my home behind too," Bradley said.

I shrugged away from him.

"It's not that I don't care," I said taking a teaspoon of offense to his words.

I'd known his family too. Bradley's mother had been as sweet as sugar and his dad always had a big grin for me whenever he saw me. Both of them had told me multiple times how good I was for Bradley.

He had a younger sister who was off at college that I met on holidays. She was perfectly nice and normal. Kind even.

"I'm just saying I know it's hard but maybe it's for the best," Bradley said.

"You want to leave?" I asked.

"Yeah, I guess." Bradley shrugged and everything about him softened. "I mean, I don't think we can stay here forever. At some point, we're going to have to risk it and maybe doing it now while we have all this stuff will give us the best shot."

I turned and looked at him. It was probably the smartest thing he'd ever said.

"What?" he asked with a grin and a chuckle.

"Nothing," I said hardening my jaw.

"No tell me," he pleaded and his smile didn't waver.

I straightened my spine as I turned away. "Maybe you're right."

"Wow," Bradley said with a laugh from deep within.

"Wow, what?" I said jolting to face him.

He wilted slightly but his jolly expression didn't change. "That's not something I ever thought I'd hear. I'm right. I like it. It sounds really good."

"I said maybe... maybe you're right."

"Close enough. I'll take it."

I shook my head as I walked away leaving him standing there grinning like a fool.

Austin eyed me as I approached. If he wanted to ask me what Bradley had said to me, he didn't.

"Are you ready?" Austin asked.

My nerves tingled and I wished he would have asked me about Bradley instead. I could feel my blood pulsing through my veins and the back of my neck rose in temperature.

Austin must have sensed my apprehension. "We don't have to do this."

I lowered my gaze to the ground before shooting a quick glance in Bradley's direction. His words echoed in the back of my mind.

"No," I said filling my lungs with oxygen. My body was overflowing with nervousness and fear, but I did all I could not to let it show. "I'm ready."

There was no place in this world for tears and fears. I had to be strong and tough with a hard shell around me always... always.

"When will they learn to shoot?" I asked. "I could use a refresher."

Austin nodded. "Hmm. Now? Maybe we shouldn't leave today."

"No," I said sharply. "We can learn as we go. We'll make stops."

"Okay," Austin said looking at me from under the brim of his hat. "Maybe an hour before we leave? Noah and I can check everything, go over the list, and eat."

It was almost as if he was asking for my permission. "Sounds good."

"Marty," Austin said before releasing a short, sharp whistle.

"Yeah?" he hollered from the lawn chair. "Time to do some training."

Marty clapped his hands abruptly as he hooted. He walked over the Bradley and slapped him on the back.

"Class is in session," Marty said loud enough for everyone to hear.

I turned to make my way over to Marty but Austin grabbed my hand and pulled me to him. My breath hitched as I slammed into his chest.

The breath I let out from between my lips was heated. He was looking at me with a passion that reminded me of our night together in my room.

It looked like he wanted to say something but his words weren't finding their way to his lips. My eyes focused on his soft lips.

Austin cleared his throat and smiled as he reluctantly took a step back. "This is frustrating."

I grinned back as I shook my head. "What is frustrating?"

"I have the girl of my dreams but I can't spend the night with her and roll out of bed at noon. Our breakfast is a stale granola bar instead of eggs and pancakes in bed," Austin said brushing his thumb across his lower lip as if he were trying to taste the warm meal. "I wish I could give you better. I wish I could give you something more."

"We're together," I said biting my lip. "I don't need more. Although eggs would be so great. So, so great."

"One day, I'll be able to give you something more," Austin said but I knew it wasn't something he could promise.

Our lives would be drastically different but that didn't mean they couldn't still be good.

"I should get going," I said holding his hand as I took a step backward. "Looks like class is about to start."

Austin tightened his fingers around mine and pulled me closer. He gave me a quick, passion filled kiss before releasing me.

I stepped away from him like I was weightless... I was a feather blowing in the wind. My insides were cotton candy and rainbows and gumdrops, right up until I caught Marty's scrunched-up face.

His eyes brows squeezed together as he looked at me with concern. "Are you going to be sick?"

I drew in a long breath and sighed still feeling Austin's lips on mine.

Marty shook his head as he handed me a gun. The cool metal popped the bubble Austin had put around me.

Dirt swirled around the rubble where the barn had once been. Reality.

Marty shook my arm.

"Hmm?" I said twisting at the waist to look at him.

"Are you sure you're up for this?"

I pressed my lips together as I swallowed hard. If there was ever going to be a chance that Austin and I were going to lazily roll out of bed on a Saturday morning at noon, we'd have to find it somewhere else. Somewhere far away from the holes in the ground. Somewhere the creatures wouldn't go.

We needed to leave. There probably wasn't much of a chance that Austin and I could have that life, but if we could, it wasn't here.

I flicked my brow upward. "I'm so ready."

CHAPTER SEVEN

As we drove away from the house, various moments from my life flashed before my eyes. I thought of summer days where the sun was so hot I could barely stand it. Marty and I would take turns spraying ourselves with the hose while dad worked in the barn.

I thought of nearly every Christmas morning I could remember. Marty and I running down the stairs to open presents. And the year dad had gotten a tree so tall we hadn't been able to put the star on top.

There had been a few times my mom had hosted Thanksgiving, cooking in the small kitchen before dad had it remodeled. Aunts, uncles, and cousins that I hadn't seen in years had come to enjoy the feast my mom had worried hadn't been good enough. There hadn't been enough butter in the potatoes or enough poultry seasoning in the stuffing, but in reality, it had been delicious and everyone wanted to come back again the following year.

Then, I thought about all the barbeques my dad had during grilling season. Though, as far as he had been concerned, it was always grilling season. I smiled at the memory.

Austin and Noah had been there even when we were younger. Those younger years we'd run around in the yard trying to catch fireflies and toads. I hadn't even remembered those moments until we were driving away from the house.

All of my good memories floated to the top of my mind and if there were bad ones, I couldn't remember them. Well, that wasn't exactly true. I could remember the most recent two that if I gave too much mental energy to, I'd probably burst into tears.

Losing your parents wasn't something you ever would get over. At least, I was almost sure that would be the case.

The visions of losing my parents would always crush the good memories out of existence. All I could do was push them away before they could erase the good ones completely.

Marty and I were with Austin in his truck. They both had the windows rolled down and their arms hanging out as if it were any other day driving down the road.

I was in the middle trying to keep my hair tucked behind my ears so it didn't blow in front of my face. Each time a strand whipped in front of me, I thought it was a creature's claw reaching toward us.

I wanted to be constantly aware of our surroundings but it was difficult. And exhausting.

As we drove into the town to pick up a few things on our way to the address Marty had found on his phone, beads of perspiration tickled the back of my neck. It was hard to believe all the destruction around us was our town.

We'd go there almost every weekend to go grocery shopping and run errands. Just off the main street, about six blocks to the south, was the high school I graduated from. My class had been a group of seventy-five and now they were probably all gone.

The buildings were nothing but half-standing walls and piles and piles of rubble. It looked like one giant junkyard.

Broken glass scattered the roads and sidewalks making everything sparkle like a fairy wonderland but what we were living in was far from anything wonderful.

Everything was gone and it had been demolished so quickly. The creatures had torn everything down until nothing worked and we'd lost communication. We'd been lucky to have electricity for as long as we had. Even if they hadn't destroyed the buildings, there would have been no one left to work in them because the relentless creatures had devoured everyone.

Noah drove my mom's SUV close to the back of Austin's truck. With how often Austin glanced back in his rearview mirror it almost seemed as if he was annoyed by just how close he was.

When I turned back to look at them over my shoulder, I could see them all gawking out of the window wearing the same shocked expression. The devastation was hard to take in... hard to believe... nearly impossible to comprehend.

"I think this used to be the grocery store, right?" Austin said pulling his truck to a stop at the curb.

Sadness wrinkled my brow. "Yeah, pretty sure this was it."

Austin sighed as he shook his head. His knuckles were white as he gripped the steering wheel.

"There's nothing left," I said worried he was going to get out and try to dig his way around.

"Yeah," he said releasing his grip on the wheel. He pulled off his hat and scratched the side of his head. "Maybe it's not going to be as easy as I thought to find supplies."

Noah walked up to Austin's window and leaned in slightly. "What's our plan here?"

"We'll take a look around, I guess," Austin said

pulling his hat back on and wiggling it until it was in perfect position. "But it doesn't look very good."

"No, no it doesn't," Noah agreed.

I chewed my cheek for a quick moment. "Are you sure about this? You guys could get hurt."

"We'll be careful," Austin said giving me a quick kiss on the cheek before opening his door and sliding out of the truck. He placed his hands on the door and locked eyes with me. "Stay in the truck."

"Of course," I said innocently.

"So bossy," Marty teased in a soft voice.

Noah waved his hand at Bradley and Mallory... a signal of some sort to indicate they should stay in the vehicle. Not that it was likely that Noah had to worry about either of them jumping out of the SUV to help them crawl around in a pile of shards and broken wood and metal.

I wondered what was going through Bradley's head as he looked at the store. Mallory was probably just glad she didn't have to call in sick.

"If every city looks like this, we're in trouble," Marty said.

He was absolutely right. It had looked like a wild pack of bulldozers had been driving about after a long night of partying.

"I don't even think it was this bad when Austin and

I came to get gas a few days ago," I said looking at the buildings behind us.

"You think it's getting worse? Why would it get worse?" Marty asked his eyes filling with worry.

"Maybe." I shrugged. "Maybe the creatures are desperate. This could be what they do to make sure they aren't missing any food."

"Food being us," Marty said twisting his fingers together.

I lowered my head but kept my eyes on Austin. "It's possible they hear things that aren't there. Or maybe they just like to destroy things. I don't think we'll ever know."

Marty's complexion paled. "We don't have a shot at surviving this, do we?"

I wanted to tell him that we'd be fine. That we'd figure it out in time but I couldn't. It felt much too close to lying and I didn't want to do that.

"I don't know what's going to happen," I said feeling as if my body was suddenly shrinking. "All we can do is try, right?"

Marty sighed. "I guess but is there any point in trying?"

Thankfully, I didn't have to answer his question because Austin and Noah were on their way back from walking around the heaps of debris. Their hands were empty which wasn't even a little surprising.

Austin climbed into the truck and turned the key. The engine roared to a noisy start.

"It's going to be okay," Austin said in a comforting tone but I wasn't exactly sure which of us he was speaking to the most. "There will be other places and we have enough food and water to last for days, maybe even weeks if we ration. We have everything we need."

"For now," Marty mumbled.

"We could dig through the rubble," Austin said as he turned the wheel, driving around an abandoned car. "It would take time we don't have right now. Noah and I both decided it makes more sense to drive as far as we can while we have the daylight hours. It might be harder to drive at night."

Marty snorted. "Even with all these lights?"

"I don't know," Austin said with a shrug. "We'll see how it goes."

I kind of wondered if maybe he was worried about his brother being separated from him during the night. I'm sure he didn't want to lose the only family he had left either.

"We probably aren't going to find anyone there when we get there anyway," Marty said. "That building probably isn't even standing anymore."

As we drove out of town, a loud noise filled the air. The three of us exchanged a confused glance and I looked up toward the sky.

It sounded like the chop-chop-chop of a helicopter above but the sky was empty except for a few scattered gray clouds.

"What is that?" Marty asked. He looked at his side mirror and his mouth dropped. "Oh shit."

I whipped my head around to try to see what Marty was seeing. The only thing I spotted was the confused faces of Bradley, Mallory and Noah looking back at me. It was clear they heard the sounds too.

The noises roared louder and my hand covered my mouth when I spotted what Marty must have seen in his mirror.

"Oh, no," I said as the gang of thirty or more motorcycles started zipping around the side of the SUV.

The motorcycles roared like angry lions as they sped by turning in front of Austin's truck. Each motorcycle was driven by a man dressed in nothing but black, some of them with what appeared to be long swords strapped to their backs.

The biker leading the way waved his hand over his head as he pressed on his brake. Austin stepped hard on the pedal to stop us from slamming into the back wheel of the man's bike.

"Dammit," Austin grumbled giving the bed of his truck a quick glance. All of our supplies were in the back, none of which we wanted to lose.

The bikers spread out in front of us making a half-circle. A gray-haired man with a long, braided beard that had been leading the group stayed on his bike. He crossed his arms as he stared at us.

He spit on the ground several feet in front of his bike before cocking his head to the side. "Step out of your vehicle."

Austin looked around as if trying to find a way to drive out of the situation. The man shook his head as if he could read Austin's mind.

He drew in a deep breath and placed his hand on my thigh. Austin didn't take his eyes off of the men in front of us.

He reached over, sliding his hand onto the door handle. "Stay in the truck." Austin swallowed so hard I thought I'd heard it. "No matter what happens, do not get out of the truck."

CHAPTER EIGHT

Austin took several steps away from the door and stopped at the front end of his truck. If he was armed, I couldn't tell.

He was trying to look casual and unafraid but I wasn't sure if it was working.

Noah didn't get out. He stayed in the SUV keeping his eyes glued to his brother. I knew they'd put several guns in the SUV but whether or not he had access to one was another story.

Even if they did have access to their guns, it wouldn't do much good. The bikers were probably armed beyond their swords too.

My stomach swirled as the biker with the braided beard made his way over to Austin. He stopped about five feet away and shifted his gaze to Marty and me before focusing on Austin again.

"What are you folks doing here?" he asked sloshing something in his mouth side to side.

"This is our town," Austin said.

"Ain't no one left in this town but us," the man said.

Austin's head bobbed up and down. "We lived out in the country. We had a farm."

"No shit?" the man said. "Which one?"

"My dad was Franklin Brown," Austin said.

The man shook his head. "Noticed you said was."

"Yeah, he didn't make it," Austin said.

"Shit," the man said spitting out a thick, brownish wad of saliva. "He was a good man. You his boy, huh? Think I see the resemblance."

Austin nodded.

"Aw man, really sorry for your loss. He stopped in my shop from time to time for repairs." The man shook his head and stuck out his hand. "Name's Jimmy."

When Austin didn't seem to recognize him, the man smiled.

"From Jimmy's Fixin' and Towing."

"Oh sure," Austin said and the two men stood there in silence.

The man took another look inside the truck. "Your dad's farm is out the other way. What you kids doing out here?"

"We were going to pick up some food in town

before leaving," Austin said shaking his head. "But everything's gone."

"Yeah, those damn things don't quit," Jimmy said. "You all hungry?"

"We're good for now," Austin said. "Was hoping to find more."

Jimmy spat again. "We don't have much or I'd offer some. I still got a lot of mouths to feed you see."

"Yeah," Austin said. "How have you been surviving?"

"Was just about to ask you the same thing," Jimmy said.

Austin shrugged. "Been lucky so far."

"Same," Jimmy chuckled. His eyes darted toward me again and I couldn't help but squirm a bit closer to Marty. "Say, we have a place at the other end of town. If you need a place to stay, we've got room."

"We appreciate at that but we really need to get on the road," Austin said.

Jimmy hesitated. It seemed as if he was considering not letting us leave.

"Where you headed?" Jimmy asked.

"We're hoping to find survivors," Austin said.

Jimmy laughed and several of the men behind him chuckled along. "You're not going to find anything out there. We went about two hundred miles in nearly every direction and it's like this everywhere."

Austin didn't respond. There was a long pause before Jimmy spit again and shifted his weight.

"Well, if you change your mind our door will be open. You know where the shop is?" Jimmy asked.

"I do," Austin nodded.

"Our place is safe. They don't like the lights, but I can see by your vehicles you've already figured that out," Jimmy said.

Austin nodded. "I appreciate it and we'll keep it in mind."

"All right," Jimmy said taking several steps closer to Austin and sticking out his hand. "We'll let you get back on your way."

"Thanks," Austin said.

The two men shook hands for a few seconds longer than what was normal. Jimmy pulled Austin closer for a second and whispered something before letting go.

He gave him a wave and Austin stood there watching as they started their bikes and drove away clearing the road. When we couldn't hear the sounds of the noisy bikes, he got back into the truck.

"That was weird," Marty said as Austin climbed back inside.

"Yeah, yeah it was," Austin said waving his hand out the window as he stepped on the accelerator. He looked into the rearview mirror as if he was checking to make sure we weren't being followed.

"Everything okay?" I asked.

Austin looked at me and then back at the road. He forced a smile before meeting my eyes again.

"Yeah, everything's fine," he said. "It's just if we have to come back, we can't come through town."

"He said that?" I asked.

"Basically. He's letting us go because he knew my dad." Austin was trying to play cool but there was a slight shakiness to his fingers that hadn't been there before. "This is their town now. Their stuff. We're lucky we didn't stick around."

Marty looked at the bed of the truck. "Guess we're also lucky they didn't check the back."

"Very lucky," Austin said. "Next time won't go as smoothly."

I looked out the window and wrapped my arms around my body. A shiver ran up and down my spine that shook my body.

"Cold?" Austin asked moving his hand near the door ready to roll up the window.

I shook my head. Maybe I was cold, but it wasn't from the temperature outside.

"We won't have connections in other towns. If survivors have already marked their territory, we're in trouble," I said.

"We'll just have to stay out of the way," Austin said.

"How do we do that when we'll need to restock our supplies?" I said patting my thighs with my palms.

Austin let out a long breath. "Marty will give more weapons training. We'll have to be ready to defend ourselves and our stuff."

"I don't know if I can do that," I said with a frown. "Sure, I can threaten people but to actually pull the trigger? I don't think that's something I could ever do."

"Hopefully, we won't have to," Austin said glancing in his rearview mirror to make sure Noah was still behind us. "Most everyone is gone. Out of everyone back home, the other survivors were us and a handful of bikers."

Marty made a strange squeaky noise. "Why the bikers?"

"No idea," Austin said. "They must have found a way just like we did."

"Well, we did it, they did it, surely there are others who did it too," I said scanning the horizon as if I'd just find more survivors glowering at us with their weapons pointed at us.

"And we're all just looking for the same thing," Austin said. "We can't assume the worst."

"Maybe we should," I countered.

Austin turned and looked at me. He kept his eyes off of the road for so long I started to get nervous.

Austin shook his head. "You're right. Dammit,

you're right." He slammed his hands against the wheel. "Shit!"

I placed my hand on his tensed bicep. I wished I could erase having voiced my worries. It hadn't done any good. The only thing it had done was to worry both Austin and Marty as well.

"Should we go back?" Austin asked slowing the truck.

There was a long pause before Marty spoke. "If there is help at the church, we'll be better off there, won't we?"

"I don't know," Austin said taking his hat off and tossing it onto the dash. He ran his hand through his hair that was slightly damp just above his ears. "I don't know anything."

It seemed as though Austin had been shaken by the bikers. The encounter had rattled his confidence.

"We're not that far," Austin said. "We could go back and plan this trip better."

"No," I said firmly. "Those bikers know you. Maybe they recognized me. They might go there. I'm not sure if we'd be safe there."

The second the words were out of my mouth, I wished I could take them back. Austin stepped on the brake. He looked down at his thighs, keeping his hands on the steering wheel with his elbows locked.

"You're right. We've essentially lost everything... because of me," Austin said.

"None of this is because of you." I rubbed his shoulder. "We all wanted to go. And we should go."

I looked out of the back window at Noah getting out of the parked SUV. He was coming to see what was wrong.

"What's going on?" Noah asked with narrowed eyes as he looked at his brother.

"I'm not sure this is the right thing," Austin said.

Noah shook his head. "What did those bikers say?"

"They knew dad, that's the only reason they let us go," Austin said.

"What does that mean exactly?" Noah asked looking at me and then at Marty. It didn't seem as though he understood what was going on.

"I don't know," Austin said. "They would have taken our stuff? Maybe even our vehicles."

I wondered if Austin knew more than he was saying.

"We can't go back," Austin said turning to look at Noah. He let his arms fall to his lap.

"Thought we were going to that church?" Noah said.

"What are we going to do if we run into something like that again? What are the six of us going to do?" Austin asked.

Noah shrugged. "We'll do what we have to do, right?" He slapped his brother on the shoulder. "Come on, man. This isn't like you. We'll be okay."

"What if I can't keep her safe," Austin blurted.

"We'll all keep each other safe," Noah said.

Austin lowered his head. I could feel everything he was feeling as if it were radiating out of him like a contagious disease. And I understood.

We hadn't been able to keep our families safe. How could we even think for a second that we could keep each other safe?

It wasn't just the creatures out there... we had to worry about other dangers as well. Desperate humans.

CHAPTER NINE

We didn't stop driving when night started to fall. Austin took a small break around dinner time, letting Marty drive his truck.

Marty sat pin straight, his hands at ten and two as he grinned the entire time. Driving Austin's truck was some kind of victory. Austin's truck was his baby and I was surprised he'd let Marty behind the wheel.

He must have been absolutely drained. I never even liked Marty driving the car we shared. He drove fast... turned sharply. Every road was a race track.

Austin wrapped his arm around my shoulders and I rested my head against the top of his chest. I tried to absorb his warmth.

There was still a pinch of sunlight on the horizon but the lights on the truck and the SUV were doing most of the work lighting the way.

"Oh, shit!" Marty said slamming on the brakes.

Behind us, the SUV screeched to a stop only inches away from Austin's bumper. Marty flashed Austin a worried look.

"I had to stop," Marty said pointing at the road. "Noah shouldn't follow so closely."

There was a large hole in the middle of the road. I was almost certain I could hear the wretched creatures releasing their sharp screeches.

"Move over," Austin said to Marty as he started climbing over me to get to the driver's seat. His masculine, woodsy scent would have made me swoon if I hadn't been worried about the hole in the road.

Marty scooted over to the middle and I was pressed against the cold door. All the warmth I'd taken from Austin gone in an instant.

I reached over and checked to make sure the door was locked because even though the area was glowing brighter than the sun, I was still terrified of the creatures.

"We'll just go around," Austin said as his phone buzzed. He picked it up and I didn't have to look to know it was Noah asking what was going on. Austin's finger moved rapidly as he typed in a quick message.

He stared at it for a moment.

"Dammit," Austin said tossing his phone roughly on the dash. "Not delivered."

"Try again," I suggested.

"Not going to bother... it's been spotty for the whole day," Austin said turning to Marty. "Don't lose that address for the church."

"I won't," Marty said. "Besides, I have it memorized."

Austin stared at him for a long moment before finally blinking to break the connection between them. It didn't seem as though he believed him but at the moment, perhaps, he didn't care.

The hole was massive. It was at least four times the size of the one I'd found at the house and probably even more massive than the one that they'd made through the basement floor of my house.

Austin turned the wheel slowly, making a large circle around the hole. We bounced a bit as the truck went halfway into the ditch as he made his way to the other side. The sounds of the creatures increased in volume and their hands reached up out of the hole like weeds waving in the breeze.

I twisted myself to look out the back window to make sure Noah was following the same path Austin had taken. Austin drove slowly down the highway as if he expected to see another hole in the road.

"Maybe we should stop for the night," Austin said.

"We're so close to that hole," Marty said running his palms up and down his thighs.

"Further ahead then," Austin said jerking his chin forward.

Marty's hands were still moving. "Those things could be all around us in the shadows."

They probably were. I couldn't see them moving and I couldn't hear them, but something told me they were out there watching us.

Every so often, I thought I'd caught a glimmer of their glowing blue eyes but I'd blink and it would be gone. It was just little flickers like fireflies on a hot July night.

"What if we could find another house," I said staring into the empty distance.

Outside of our globe of light, there wasn't anything out there. There was a moon above and stars that twinkled, both reminding me that we were still on earth. Everything beyond that was a blank canvas at night, or maybe it would be more accurate to call it a black hole.

"There's nothing left standing," Marty said.

"Our house was... maybe we could find another," I said. "If something in the middle of nowhere had been abandoned, maybe we could make it our own."

I could feel Marty's eyes on me. "You don't want to see what's at this church?"

"I guess I do," I said with a shrug. "But we should have a backup plan, right? Maybe we could build our own place with all the wood around."

"I don't see how that's even remotely safe," Marty said.

I lowered my voice trying to keep the hopelessness out of it. "There isn't anywhere that is safe."

"It's not a bad idea," Austin said. "We know the light will keep us safe."

"But we can't light the ground below whatever we build." Marty threw his hands into the air. "They'll just dig through and get us just like they got mom."

"There has to be something we can do to protect us," I said. "The bikers are doing it. The people in the church are doing it. Maybe there is something we're missing."

Marty shook his head. "They've just been lucky so far, just like we'd been. I'm sure their time will come."

"It won't hurt to try," I said sourly.

"We'll try the church first, then, if we need to, we'll find a place to rebuild," Austin said. "While we're making our way, we can think about our backup plan." He looked at me from across the truck. "Okay?"

"Yeah, sounds good," I said forcing a thin-lipped smile.

The more time we spent outside, the more I realized how unprepared we were. What we were going through wasn't something anyone could ever be prepared for.

I didn't know how in the hell I was going to take

care of Marty. It was like we were all delicious fresh meat dangling down just above the holes. We'd bounce up and down just ever so slightly out of their reach, but one of these times the creatures would get us.

It was just after midnight according to the numbers on the clock. There were far too many hours of darkness left and I didn't know what to do to stop myself from having a panic attack.

My heart was racing and my breathing was quickening. Marty looked at me cocking his head to the side.

"Are you okay?" he asked.

"Yeah," I said in an odd squeaky voice.

"You sound just like I do right before I start hyperventilating," Marty said with a chuckle. He stiffened and then turned to me. "Oh, shit, you're not going to, are you?"

I held up my palm taking in breaths that made my lungs feel like they were being stabbed with a dull blade. My fingers wrapped around the armrest tingling with numbness.

"I'm fine," I said releasing a breath as calmly as I could manage between my lips.

I wasn't going to hyperventilate, it was the truth, but a panic attack? That was possible. And even likely if I didn't pull it together.

I cleared my throat. "I think we should keep going.

We can go slow, but we should keep going, don't you think?"

The words flowed out of my mouth like rain down the window pane during a thunderstorm. If I hadn't pressed my lips together, I probably would have still been talking.

"Yeah," Austin said in a tone that was comforting but one that didn't hide the fact that he was worried. He light jabbed Marty with his elbow. "See if you can send a message to Noah. Let him know."

Marty nodded as he powered on his phone. "Will do."

He typed in the message and the word sending appeared. It stayed on the screen for a long moment before it showed that the message hadn't been delivered.

Marty sighed but he tried to resend. And even after the sixth failed attempt, he didn't stop trying.

CHAPTER TEN

When the sun came up, Austin stopped the truck. We were in the middle of nowhere.

There were trees on the left side of the round and to our right was a long fence along the road that appeared to have once gone around a field. If there had been a farm, it was no longer there.

The birds in the trees sang and tweeted back and forth likely talking about the strangers in their area. Or maybe they were trying to warn us about what was lurking inside the dark woodsy area below them.

We all gathered at the back of Austin's truck to stretch our legs. Mallory was the only one who didn't have eyelids that were half closed.

Austin dug around and pulled out several bottles of water and a couple boxes of toaster pastries. I knew I should eat but my stomach felt like it was shrinking into itself.

"We're going to have to stop for a break," Austin said and everyone bobbed their head in agreement.

I wasn't exactly sure how I felt but I knew it wouldn't be safe to keep going with nearly everyone half asleep. I didn't want to stop. Driving at night was slow and terrifying. During the day, we could go faster and make much better time but it wouldn't be worth it if someone fell asleep at the wheel.

"I was hoping you'd say that," Noah said rubbing the corner of his eye with a knuckle. "So damn exhausted."

"I could drive," Mallory said with a casual shrug.

Austin and Noah exchanged a quick glance. I didn't need to be a mind reader to know that just wasn't an option. Oddly Mallory had picked up on it, too.

"Don't be like that," Mallory said puffing out her lower lip. "I can drive just fine. I've never been in an accident."

"It's time for a break," Austin said.

Mallory crossed her arms. "I have to pee."

Austin held up a finger and reached into the back of the truck. He opened one of the tied-up garbage bags and pulled out a roll of toilet paper. He tossed it in her direction.

Mallory stepped to the side as if he were tossing her a dead rat. She looked down at it and after a moment squeezed her eyebrows together.

"Lucy?" she said sweetly.

My eyes widened as she picked up the roll of toilet paper. I already knew what she was going to ask and I was trying with all my might to think of an excuse.

"Come with me?" she asked as she tugged on my arm.

I bit my lip. "Oh, I'm not sure if I should."

"I don't want to go alone," Mallory whined.

I turned to Bradley as if he should be the one going with his fiancé.

"Fine," I groaned as I looked into the bed of the truck. I wanted to take something with me — a weapon — just in case.

"What are you doing?" she asked as I leaned over the side of the truck.

I didn't answer as I grabbed my dad's shotgun from the back and his heavy-duty flashlight from the cab.

"We're going to need that?" Mallory said pointing at the gun.

I shrugged and gestured for her to lead the way. She gingerly walked across the road looking from side to side as if she were worried the creatures would create a new hole at her feet.

I glanced over my shoulder at the others as we

stepped down into the squishy ditch. There was a slight incline as we made our way into the trees.

The birds above us ceased their chirps but it seems as though the ones in the distance became more vocal. It felt like the temperature inside the trees dropped at least ten degrees.

"Okay," I said firmly planting my feet in a dry spot of dirt.

"They can still see me," Mallory said.

I turned my back to her. "No, they can't and trust me, they don't care to see."

"I just like my privacy is all," Mallory said.

I wanted to tell her everyone does, but I didn't want the conversation to continue. It was like being in a random women's restroom and having someone try to strike up a conversation with you from the other stall.

I leaned against a tree keeping my back to Mallory as I watched Noah and Bradley climb back into the SUV. Noah reclined the driver's seat and pulled his hat down over his eyes.

Austin gave a quick glance in our direction before leaning against the back of the truck. He said something to Marty and Marty nodded before walking around to the front of the truck. He disappeared from view as he laid down on the front seat.

I shook my head even though they couldn't see me.

Austin was the one that should have been lying down on the seat getting his rest.

A group of small birds released a chorus of anxious chirping sounds. It sounded like they were hungry and waiting for their mother to return with their breakfast.

Mallory let out a terrified scream from behind me and when I turned, I realized the noises hadn't come from baby birds at all. There were three miniature sized creatures hopping through the trees at a quick pace as they made their little high-pitched squeaks.

Mallory's feet look like they were moving through pudding as she tried to get to me.

"Lucy! Help!" she called with wide, saucer eyes.

The little creatures bounced around heading in her general direction but they bumped clumsily into nearly every tree along the way. They didn't have the skills of the larger creatures but that didn't stop them from trying to hunt their prey.

Mallory crawled to me and grabbed my leg. "Help!"

"Come on," I said swinging the gun over my shoulder to help her to her feet. We had to get out of the shade of the trees.

My eyes scanned the area looking for the larger creatures that would be accompanying the smaller ones but I couldn't find any. Perhaps the smaller ones were braver. Maybe their eyes just weren't as sensitive to the light as the grown creatures.

The little creatures were even more inaccurate than the grown ones but they were faster. Somewhere in the distance or maybe even from down below, a creature let out a painful high-pitched squeal.

I pulled Mallory's arm but instead of her moving along with me, she crashed to the ground with a surprised gasp. There was a small creature perched upon her back ready to dig its claws into her body.

I used the flashlight and smacked the thing on the side of the head. It whimpered as it rolled off of Mallory and onto the ground next to her. She moved faster than I thought possible as she crawled toward the road.

I followed her reaching down to help her to her feet. Right as I bent over, a second creature had launched itself at me. It slammed into a tree to my left, missing the back of my neck by just inches.

"Dammit," I breathed.

Mallory screamed as the third one made its attempt. It stopped in its tracks and covered its ears.

The hesitation was enough for me to click the flashlight on and aim the beam directly into its eyes. It whined and ran off bumping into several trees along the way.

I breathed heavily trying to keep the oxygen

flowing through my body so I didn't fall into having a complete panic attack. My eyes darted around as I looked for the other two creatures to flash the beam into their eyes.

Mallory cried out a random noise and turned and ran out of the trees. I backed out of the trees slowly moving the flashlight in every direction possible as I grabbed the gun in my left hand.

The light had worked well enough on the small creature but that didn't mean I didn't want to have the shotgun ready. If the parent of the small creature came looking for me, I wanted to be ready. I'd scream just like Mallory had as I flashed it in the eyes with the light, and if none of that worked, well, I'd shoot it in the face.

I backed away, releasing sharp gasps as I looked at each shadow expecting something to jump out at me. There were too many shadows... too many hiding spots. I couldn't find them all and I definitely couldn't watch them all at the same time.

My breath got stuck inside my throat as I back into something. I turned so quickly I felt lightheaded.

The flashlight was up and the bright light was in the eyes staring back at me. I couldn't breathe. I couldn't move and I was just about to scream, but before I could, a hand covered my mouth.

Austin's eyes were wide, pleading with mine to

recognize that it was him staring at him. It took me what felt like several minutes.

I let him drag me across the street and away from the trees. The muscles in my legs had turned into putty.

He said the same words over and over to me but they hadn't made sense. They were just words.

Austin held me. "It's going to be okay."

The rest of the day we all took turns driving. Marty and I each drove for as long as we could keep our eyes open. We planned to wait as long as possible before waking Austin. He needed the rest more than any of us because I knew after what had happened, he would want to be the one driving at night.

Mallory had been so shaken by what had happened, she probably wouldn't ever get out of the SUV again. It wasn't like I was handling what happened all that much better. My fingers were wrapped so tightly around the steering wheel that it wasn't just my knuckles that were white.

"You're driving so slow," Marty said.

"Oh, sorry," I said looking at the speedometer.

He was right. I was only going thirty-five miles per

hour on a road that was completely free of any abandoned cars or debris.

"I wish the GPS on your phone was working," I said. "It would be nice to know how close we are to the church."

"Yeah, and I could know how much time I have to prepare," Marty said.

"Prepare?" I asked. "What do you need to prepare for?"

He looked out of the window off to the right as if he were hiding his face from me. "I guess I thought I wanted to go but now I'm not so sure."

"What changed your mind?" I asked.

If anything, after the baby creature attack, I was actually looking forward to getting out of the truck and hiding in a building for a while.

"I haven't changed my mind, it's just more that I have no idea what the right thing to do is," Marty admitted.

"None of us do," I said chuckling softly. "I have absolutely no idea what the right thing is but I also don't think we have a lot of options. If mom and dad were still here, they'd know."

It was Marty's turn to laugh. He glanced at me out of the corner of his eye before shaking his head.

"They wouldn't have known what to do either,"

Marty said. "It's probably better that they aren't here to see us die."

I opened my mouth but then my mind went blank. Maybe he was right. Maybe they were better off.

"You want me to take a turn?" Marty offered clearly wanting to change the subject.

"Nah, I'm good for a bit longer. Get some rest," I said.

"You sure?" Marty asked nudging me with his elbow. "You look tired."

I rolled my eyes. "We all look tired." I glanced at him noticing the red spiderwebs in the whites of his eyes. "Really, I'm fine. Get some rest."

Each passing mile became more challenging but I had my mind made up that I was going to drive as long as I possibly could. The adrenaline pumping through my veins was wearing off, but there was still enough of it there to keep my eyes open.

There hadn't been anything to see in miles. A few broken-down homes, fields that hadn't been tended to, and various groupings of trees. Every time we drove through a section of the road that cut between the trees, I was ready for a pack of baby creatures to pounce out and land on the truck. Hell, I probably should have turned the lights on because of the shadows, but I didn't bother.

It only seemed as though the younger creatures

had been out in the shadows. Their parents had been calling for them to come back from below.

It was a frightening thought really because when the babies grew up, they'd be less afraid. They wouldn't stay below the surface during the day. A day might come where we'd have to worry about the shadows... if we ever made it to that day.

We hadn't stopped for a break since the baby creature attack but I knew we'd have to stop soon. I just kept telling myself that I could make it one more mile and before I'd known it, we'd gone an additional twenty miles.

I was excited. We were making good time even though I was driving a little slowly.

Behind Austin's truck, Bradley was driving my mom's SUV. Every so often, I'd look into the rearview mirror at him clutching the wheel and staring straight ahead. He seemed nervous. Uncomfortable. I wasn't sure if it was because he didn't want to drive or because of what happened to Mallory and me.

Marty shifted in his seat and groaned. "You need to go faster."

I had thought he'd been asleep.

"Sorry," I grumbled as I pressed down on the accelerator.

"We're never going to get there at this rate," Marty mumbled. It didn't sound like he was fully awake.

"Okay, okay, sorry!" I said waving my hand at him even though he probably had his eyes closed. It wasn't like I needed help driving. "Go back to sleep."

He shifted around for another minute or so before his head fell back and rested to the side. His mouth dropped open and he released a nearly completely inaudible snore.

Marty's sleep was restless. It seemed as though he was dreaming about something and I could only guess that it was something similar to the nightmares I had when I closed my eyes.

Austin probably had them, too. We probably all did.

A yawn so large it pulled my lips apart so far it felt like the corners were going to crack. I was exhausted even though the adrenaline was still surging through my veins.

I forced my eyes open wider because even if I woke Marty for his turn, I knew that I wouldn't be able to fall asleep anyway. There was just too much going on in my head for my mind to let me relax enough to find sleep.

The yawns kept coming with each mile. My speed dropped slower but I managed to go faster than what I'd been doing when Marty told me to speed up.

For a second, everything had gone black. My eyes popped open and I coughed to cover my gasp. It had been a long blink. But the blink had definitely been too long.

I told myself one more mile. I could do one more mile. Then, we'd be that much closer.

Except, I'd been wrong. I wasn't exactly sure what had happened but the right front tire hit the gravel and bounced the truck to the side.

I turned the wheel to get back to the road but it was no use. The truck flew into the ditch and we fishtailed as I tried to regain control.

I pressed on the brake but it wasn't the brake that stopped us. Our bodies all jerked forward at the same moment. The left front end of the truck slammed into a tree I hadn't even seen.

CHAPTER TWELVE

I felt lightheaded and disoriented. Had I hit the window with my head?

"Is everyone okay?" I asked sounding as if I had just woken up from a deep sleep. My voice was raspy and it felt as though it had been far away from my body.

Noah was at the passenger side of the truck, knocking on the window. He reached down and tried to wiggle the door open.

How had Noah gotten to us so fast? I'd only just hit the tree seconds ago, hadn't I?

Bradley was opening my door and reaching into the truck to help me down to the ground.

"I'm fine," I said swatting at his hands like they were pesky flies. I turned to Marty to drag him out of the truck with me. "Marty!"

His eyes were closed. I shook him vigorously.

"Marty, wake up!" I shouted at his face with desperation dripping from my tone.

He turned his head slightly. "No, mom," he groaned as he half-lifted his hand off of his leg. "I'm too sick to get up for work today."

"Marty, it's me," I said shaking him again.

"Stop shaking me," he said opening his eyes.

I gave him a hug and spotted Austin over his shoulder. He wasn't moving. Blood was dripping down from his eyebrow rolling down the side of his face.

"Austin," Noah said patting his palm on Austin's cheek.

He didn't open his eyes. His body was slumped to the side and it looked like Noah was supporting his weight so he didn't fall out of the truck.

"Austin!" I said practically climbing over Marty to get to him.

"I think he hit his head," Noah said glancing at me. "He's breathing. He's just out."

Noah looked at me and studied me for a long moment.

"Remember what happened?" Noah asked.

I shook my head slightly. "Not exactly. How do we wake him up?"

I was trying not to freak out but I was on the edge of a complete meltdown. If anything had happened to

Austin, I wouldn't be able to deal with it. How had I been so careless?

Noah ignored my question and kept tapping him on the cheek. "Come on, Austin," he begged. "Time to wake up, brother."

I exhaled a shaky breath just as Austin's head lifted slightly before rolling back to the side. It was like his head was too heavy for his neck to hold.

Austin's eyelids squeezed together as he pushed through the pain. He pressed his hand to his forehead just above the cut.

"Ow," Austin moaned. He looked dazed as his eyes moved around the area. He sucked in a breath when his eyes connected with mine. "You okay?"

He must have realized what had happened.

"Yeah, yeah, I'm fine," I said smiling as I placed my hand on his shoulder. "Are you okay?"

"My head is killing me," Austin said. "But otherwise, yeah, I think I am."

The confusion was pouring out of his eyes. He blinked several times focusing on the tree that the front bumper had smashed into.

"I'm so sorry about your truck," I said.

"It's just a truck," Austin said. "I'm just glad you're okay. What happened?"

My teeth dug into the inside of my cheek so hard I

thought I broke through. "I think I drifted off for a second. It was only for a second. I'm so, so sorry."

"You should have woke me up," Marty said.

"Thanks," I said. "Helpful."

A squeal from not too far off sliced through the air causing us all to freeze. Noah reached under Austin's arm to help him out of the truck.

"We should get back to the road," Bradley said from behind me.

It felt like he was too close but when I turned, he was several feet away with Marty standing next to him. They both stared at me with concern in their eyes.

A jolt of pain shot up the back of my neck like and it instantly felt as though I had a kink. I climbed out of the truck as I dug my fingertips into my bruised feeling skin.

"What about all our supplies?" I asked looking over my shoulder as we all walked through the tall grasses to the SUV.

"I'll figure it out," Noah said. "For now, let's just get back to the SUV."

Austin wrapped his arm around my shoulder. The blood was starting to dry on the side of his face.

"Did we bring a first aid kit?" I asked shaking my head. "I should know the answer to that."

"Yeah," Noah said. "It's in the SUV."

I felt tears bubbling up inside my eyes. I tried to fight them off but it felt like they were going to burn right through if I didn't let the coolness of my tears out.

"Hey," Austin said stopping to turn me to face him. "No need for that."

"I wrecked your truck," I sobbed. "I could have killed us."

"You were going like ten miles per hour, you weren't going to kill anyone," Marty said. "Even the bugs had a chance to land safely on the hood instead of getting squashed on the windshield."

I pressed my hand to my mouth. "It's my fault this happened. I could have lost both of you."

"We're fine," Marty said.

I hated that I felt so weak. Marty was staring at me. He blinked several times before smiling.

"Come on, Lucy," Marty said. "It's okay."

I couldn't cry. Not in front of Marty. I needed to be strong. He needed me to be tough.

I wiped the tears away with the back of my hand. "I must have hit my head harder than I thought."

Mallory hadn't bothered to get out of the SUV but she did open the door as we approached.

"Are you guys okay?" she asked with both concern and surprise in her voice. "I saw it all happen. It was so scary for me to watch because there wasn't anything we could do to help."

"Yeah," I said. "That must have been so hard for you."

Mallory nodded vigorously as she waved me inside. "You should sit down."

I hadn't realized until she patted the seat next to her just how unsteady my legs felt. Even though she believed the world revolved around her, she was right, I did need to sit down.

"Thanks," I said feeling as if I were shrinking as I crawled into the familiar SUV.

I wrapped my arms around my still shaking body as Bradley and Marty climbed into the back seat. The door was still open so I could hear Noah and Austin whispering.

"What about all the stuff?" I asked looking at Marty over my shoulder.

"They're thinking about driving back to that motel a quarter of a mile back to let us rest while they figure out how to pack it all in here."

"Motel?" I asked.

"Oh, that's right. You must not have seen it because you were sleeping," Marty said. His lip curled at the end revealing the slight amusement he felt at his words.

Bradley jabbed his elbow into him and shot him a look. I wanted to tell Bradley to mind his own business but the words wouldn't find their way out of my mouth. There was a small part of me that was happy he'd done it because I didn't find any humor in the situation.

I'd never been in an accident before and what made it worse was that I was driving. I should have known better.

Austin and Noah walked off back down toward the truck. They both studied the front end of the truck where I'd hit the tree.

It felt like I started shrinking again. Mallory rubbed my shoulder.

"I was in an accident once," she said. "Actually several."

I turned to look at her.

"Yeah, I was." She must have thought I hadn't believed her or that I wanted to know more. "Once I rear-ended a really old gray-haired lady. She was so sweet." Mallory leaned closer. "She wanted to make sure I was okay."

Austin climbed behind the wheel and it looked like he was trying to start the truck. Noah tried to open the hood but he couldn't get it to budge.

"Thankfully, I was fine," Mallory said. "This extremely hot paramedic checked me out and gave me the okay before handing me his number." She flapped her hand at Bradley. "Don't worry, Babe, this was like a week before I met you." Mallory frowned. "They took the woman away in an ambulance."

"Great story," Marty muttered.

"I'm trying to help your sister realize that accidents happen," Mallory said placing her hand on the seat behind her. It looked like she wanted to reach out and pet Marty. "It must have been hard for you too."

Marty puffed out his lower lip. "Yeah, it was so scary." He frowned. "Actually, I'd been asleep. It was just kind of disorienting."

It had seemed like Marty was going to mess with her but then he became serious when he thought about what had happened.

"I'm so sorry, Marty," I said biting my cheek.

Marty chuckled realizing he'd gotten too serious. "I'm fine, Lucy. The truck got the worst of it."

"And Austin's head," Bradley added. I didn't even have the energy to shoot him a razor-sharp look.

I'd managed to destroy Austin's truck and his head all at once.

Austin and Noah made their way back to the SUV, each making quick looks back at the truck. I lowered my face down into my hands.

My body jerked when my door closed abruptly. Austin had closed the door before sliding into the passenger seat. Noah was walking around the front end of the SUV, his eyes scanning the horizon. It was evident that he was worried about the number of daylight hours that were remaining.

Noah started the SUV and turned around heading back to the motel I couldn't even remember having seen.

CHAPTER THIRTEEN

The motel had mostly been destroyed. It appeared as though each room had been in its own cabin-like building. The last of which, room ten, still had all of the walls still standing but a large hole in the roof.

There were two beds that were covered with dust and dirt. Mallory was ecstatic that the bathroom door was still in place and that it was lockable.

"And it flushes!" she clapped as she stepped out giving herself a long glance in the mirror as she passed by.

"We can't stay in here when it's dark," I said crossing my arms.

"We'll be back before dark," Austin said placing a kiss on my forehead.

I wanted to tell him I was nervous about him taking the SUV and therefore the lights but I didn't want to stop him from going back to his truck. They left us with two guns and two flashlights before driving off.

He hadn't even bothered to clean the blood off his face although he had taken a bandage from the first aid kit and placed it over the small cut near his eyebrow. They were in too big of a hurry to worry about a little blood.

Marty pulled the bedspread off of the beds. "Anyone tired?"

"That bed looks amazing," Mallory said placing her fingertips on the top of her chest displaying her manicure that was still in nearly impeccable shape. "And that's from someone that only stayed in nice hotels."

Marty gestured for her to take one. "Might as well get some shut-eye while we have the chance."

"I didn't get much rest after what happened to Lucy and me," Mallory said looking at the bed as if it were a long lost lover from a past life. She inched closer and closer, sighing when she lowered herself down onto the mattress.

"Lucy?" Marty asked gesturing to the other bed.

I shook my head. "Go ahead. I can't sleep like this."

There wasn't a door to close behind me as I walked out of the room leaving the three of them alone. I sat down on the concrete in the middle of the parking lot. I pulled my legs to my chest and held myself tightly as if I was afraid I might fall apart.

Because of what I'd done, we'd all have to squeeze into the SUV. How could I have been so careless?

There wasn't anything around us for as far as I could see. It looked like maybe there had a been a gas station across the road but if there had been, now it was nothing but a pile of rubble.

In a few places, there was a scattering of trees and shrubs but nothing so thick that I was worried about what might be lurking. Where I was sitting, I'd see anything coming our way unless it soundlessly walked up behind me, but I didn't think that was likely.

The creatures weren't soundless. They made their noises so they could tell where they were going. Even the small ones had made their own little chirping noises.

I didn't hear anything except for the endless thoughts circling through my mind. The devil on my shoulder wanted to be sure I knew how badly I'd screwed everything up.

I wasn't sure how long I'd been sitting there alone when I heard the noises of the gravel crunching behind me. The steps were calm and careful. Someone was approaching and they were trying not to startle me.

"Hey," Bradley said coming to a stop at my side.

He crossed his arms and gazed out toward where

Austin and Noah were working on transferring our supplies.

"I probably should have gone with them," Bradley said glancing down at me. "But I figured they wouldn't have wanted me along."

I shrugged, but he was right. They probably wouldn't have.

"They probably would have appreciated the offer," I said.

"I suppose so," Bradley said lowering himself down next to me. He picked up a small pebble and rolled it between his fingers. "They're sleeping. If you want, you could try to get some rest."

I shook my head. It was weird but it was the first time since seeing Bradley again after everything, I didn't mind talking to him. He wasn't being a creep. He was being the Bradley I knew when we were alone in our living room and he wasn't trying to impress anyone.

"I'm not tired," I said. If Marty would have been there, he would have made a joke about me having already had my turn when I drove Austin's truck into the tree.

I groaned and rubbed the back of my neck.

"Everything okay?" Bradley asked.

I wanted to make some kind of comment about how I knew he didn't give a crap about me but somehow I managed to keep it inside.

"Yeah," I said turning to meet his eyes. "I just feel like a... a jerk. I messed everything up."

"No, you didn't," Bradley said looking at the pebble between his fingers. "I like that we'll all be together."

I hadn't given it much thought because I'd been with Austin and Marty. It wasn't like I cared about being with Bradley or Mallory but I was sure Austin hadn't liked being separated from his brother.

"Having two vehicles was better than one," I said raising my chin. I thought I'd heard an engine but I didn't see them coming down the road.

"It was awful watching the truck go into the ditch knowing you were inside," Bradley said. I could feel him inch closer. "Mallory would be dead in those trees if it hadn't been for you."

"You're giving me far too much credit for that," I said feeling a tightness at the back of my throat.

Bradley shook his head. "I'm not. All I could think about when the truck hit the tree was you."

"Bradley," I said holding up my hand.

"What? I don't get to say how I feel? I understand you're with Austin or whatever, but that doesn't mean I should have to just step back and watch you make a mistake," Bradley said.

"That's exactly what you need to do," I said

pressing my palms down onto the pavement. "More importantly, Austin is not a mistake."

Bradley shook his head and laughed. "It looks like a mistake to me. Every time you two are together you're just arguing."

"We are not!" I said my eyes lit up.

"Seems that way to me," Bradley said with a shrug.

"You are pretty much the last person in the world that should be giving relationship advice," I said pushing myself to my feet.

Bradley was on his almost as quickly. His eyes glinted with the last remaining bits of sunlight.

"I'm sorry," he said. "Jesus, Lucy, I am so sorry. I would do anything to make it up to you, anything."

"Bradley, just stop it," I said pressing my fists into my thighs.

He held up his hands as his eyes filled with defeat. Bradley lowered his head and let out a heavy sigh.

"I just wish I could get you to understand," Bradley said.

"I understand everything just fine. You need to accept that I'm with Austin," I said letting the tension building up in my muscles relax.

Bradley's shoulders drooped. "I'd do anything, for just one more night with you."

"It's not going to happen," I said chuckling as I took a step back.

Bradley matched my movement and wrapped his arms around my waist. "Look into my eyes. Tell me that you don't feel anything for me."

"I'm feeling a lot of anger," I said between my teeth.

"Lucy, I'm scared. I can't lose you again," Bradley said.

He pulled me closer and pressed his lips to mine. I pushed as hard as I could on his shoulders to break free from his hold.

"Stop it!" I said wiping my mouth with the back of my hand. "You can't just do something like that."

"Does that mean—"

"It means nothing. Go back inside," I said pointing my finger at the little number ten on the exterior wall. "Don't ever do that again, okay?"

Bradley opened his mouth to say something but the fire in my eyes had made him change his mind. He turned and stopped for a moment but then continued on.

Marty was standing about ten feet away from the cabin staring at us. He kept his eyes on Bradley as he walked by. It wasn't until Bradley was in the room that he made his way over to me.

"What was that all about?" Marty asked.

"I don't want to talk about it," I said wrapping my arms around my middle.

Marty looked down the road. "You don't have to. I practically heard everything. Mallory might have too."

"Shit," I said biting my tongue as if I could hear my mom scolding me for cursing.

"Are you going to tell Austin?" Marty asked.

I shook my head.

Marty's head bobbed up and down. "Okay. Then, I will."

CHAPTER FOURTEEN

"Marty, no!" I said grabbing his arm much too tightly.

"Why the hell not?" Marty asked his face contorted. "He needs to know."

I was pleading with my glassy eyes. "It'll just cause problems. We don't need any more trouble, Marty."

"I don't like this," Marty said shaking his head as the SUV came rolling down the road.

Even though the sun was still out, it wouldn't be for long. Noah had the SUV lit up and it looked like a fireball traveling down the road.

They pulled into the parking lot, slowing as they drove past us and right up to the cabin before shifting into park. The back of the SUV was packed so tightly I couldn't even see into the window.

"You need to talk to him," Marty said.

"Mind your own business," I said and it was like I'd lit a firecracker with a short fuse.

Marty jogged away from me heading right for the passenger door. I tried to catch up but it was too late. Austin was already asking Marty what was going on and shooting quick glances in my direction.

"Where is he?" Austin said between his teeth. He looked like he was going to explode.

"Austin, wait," I said moving my feet quicker.

He looked at me. He watched me and there was no doubt in my mind that he saw the look on my face.

But Austin didn't wait. He stepped around Marty and walked right into cabin ten.

My breath caught in my throat as I watched him carry Bradley out of the room. His fingers gripped his collar tightly as he pushed him in front of him.

There was nothing but rage in Austin's eyes. He looked like a different person... a person I'd never seen before.

Austin let go and shoved Bradley hard. Bradley stumbled backward but he managed to keep himself upright until Austin gave him another push.

Bradley crashed to the ground and scraped up a handful of pebbles. He threw them at Austin's legs.

"What's your problem, man?" Bradley said his eyes on fire.

"I was hoping you'd ask," Austin said practicing spitting the words at him.

Mallory howled from the cabin and covered her mouth. Noah stepped in front of her to block her way.

"Bradley!" she cried.

"It's fine, Mallory," Bradley said his voice wavering. "Go back inside."

Austin leaned closer to Bradley. "Why don't you tell her what you did?"

"What did I do?" Bradley said holding his hands up innocently.

"You put your hands on my girlfriend," Austin said his hand balled up into tight fists. "What kind of man does that?"

Bradley looked like he was going to burst into tears but the looked faded and he started laughing.

"You don't deserve her," Bradley said.

My mouth dropped and I looked over at Mallory who was still standing there watching. It looked like someone had stepped up behind her and thrust a long knife between her shoulder blades.

"What do you even know about her?" Bradley asked.

"I know enough not to blow my chance by sleeping with another woman," Austin said.

Heat filled my cheeks like I'd stepped inside an oven.

"Okay, enough," I said but it seemed as though I could have been invisible as far as either Bradley or Austin were concerned.

"I want you gone," Austin said. "You're not welcome here."

Bradley's eyes widened with disbelief. "What? You can't do that!"

"I can and I will," Austin said.

"That's no different from killing me," Bradley said. "Why not just be a man and do it yourself then?"

Austin smirked as he shook his head. "You made your bed. Now, lay in it."

"Austin," I said softly. "You can't do this."

Mallory was sobbing uncontrollably. "Please stop doing this!"

There was so much pain on her face. I could see it across the parking lot. It was sad that she was the one being punished.

"Austin!" I said with a hardness that made him realize I was there. He looked through his rage and saw us all staring at him.

"What?" Austin asked wiping at the side of his mouth with the back of his hand. "You think he deserves to be here?"

"I don't know what he deserves, but we can't send him away," I said holding my palms up. "He's an idiot, but he doesn't deserve to die."

"Yeah, I'm really sorry," Bradley said. "I didn't get how serious things were between you two. I'll back off. Never again."

Austin stared at him for a long moment. I knew he wanted nothing more than to send him away with nothing but the shirt on his back... if even that.

And now that we didn't have the truck we were all going to be stuck together with tempers flaring.

Austin's muscles didn't relax. He pointed at Bradley. "Get up."

Bradley looked at me as if I would tell him what to do. Austin stepped in front of me blocking his view.

"Get up," Austin repeated.

"Can I stay?" Bradley asked.

"Jesus," Austin said with a chuckle. "Get. Up."

Bradley slowly got to his feet. He looked like a turtle that wanted to hide in its shell.

"What are you going to do?" Bradley asked.

Austin raised his fist and threw it into Bradley's cheek with so much force it knocked him off his feet.

"Austin!" I said pushing him aside.

I knelt down next to Bradley and watched his eyelids fluttering as he tried to open his eyes.

"You didn't have to do that," I said looking up at Austin over my shoulder. The regret was painted on his face and pulling his shoulders down.

"I... I'm sorry," Austin said. "Shit."

Bradley's eyes opened and instantly connected with mine. There was a strange glint deep inside that made me narrow my eyes, but before I could give it much thought, Mallory pushed me out of the way.

"Are you okay?" she asked as she looked Bradley over.

"I'm sorry," Austin said but I wasn't exactly sure who he was talking to.

Mallory turned to him poison floating from her eyes. "Are you?"

"I am," Austin said before kicking the gravel and walking away.

"I'm sure he—"

"Who asked you?" Mallory said aiming her glare at me. "Why did you have to do this?"

My mouth dropped. I looked at Bradley waiting for him to say something but he didn't.

"This isn't my fault," I said I said staring at her with disbelief. "Did you hear any of what happened?"

"I heard enough," she said raising her nose to the sky... a sky that was darkening rapidly. "He was my fiancé. If you wouldn't have forced your way back into his life, none of this would have happened."

"Forced my way?" I asked taking a step back. I felt like throwing my fist in her pretty little face. I looked at Bradley and stared into his eyes. "You better tell her or I won't stop Austin from kicking you to the curb."

Mallory held up her hand. "I don't want to hear anything. Bradley and I can work through anything, isn't that right Bradley?"

"Sure," Bradley said attempting to sit up.

Noah was behind me tapping me on the shoulder.

"What?" I spat taking my frustration out on him. I sighed and thankfully he took it as an apology.

"I think you should talk to Austin," he said but what he really wanted was to separate me from Mallory.

"Yeah," I said stiffening my jaw as I gave Bradley a final look. "Fix this."

Bradley nodded and I turned my back. I already knew he wasn't going to do anything but spin things to make it look like he was the good guy. And Mallory was dumb enough to believe it.

CHAPTER FIFTEEN

The group of us stayed near the SUV during the night. Mallory and Bradley kept to themselves but since they had to stay in the light, it felt as though they were too close.

They would whisper. I could tell that Mallory was sad and it didn't seem like she liked being sad.

Bradley's cheek was black and blue where Austin had hit him. The regret practically flowed out of Austin's pores.

Noah and Austin stood apart holding their guns as they stared into the darkness. The creatures were out there making their noises, talking about us. Probably trying to come up with a plan to get us.

"Should we go?" Noah asked Austin as he paced closer to him. "I could drive."

"Do we even know if we're on the right track?"

Austin asked quietly. "We haven't seen a road sign in miles."

Noah nodded. "Marty was able to get a map on his phone. I think we could be there by morning."

Austin scratched the back of his head. "It would be better to arrive during the day."

"Should we run it by the others? See what they want to do?" Noah asked.

"No," Austin said clenching his fists. "I don't care what they want to do."

My eyes narrowed and looked down at my shoes. I wasn't supposed to be listening, at least I didn't think I was supposed to.

"You don't care what we want to do?" I asked cursing myself for having such a big mouth.

"I care what you want to do," he jerked his chin in Bradley's direction, "but I don't care what he wants to do. I have one job and that is to keep us safe."

"He's not a threat to our safety," I said straightening my spine.

It was instantly apparent that he wasn't thrilled at my response. "Now, you're on his side?"

"Austin stop it, you know I'm not. He got the message loud and clear," I said turning as Mallory marched over to us.

She stopped and placed her hands on her hips as she gave us each a look that could have started a fire.

"You will all be pleased to know that Bradley and I broke up," Mallory announced loudly as she turned to me. "Thanks to you."

"To me?" I said letting my mouth fall open. "I think you have the wrong idea. I don't have any interest in Bradley."

"It doesn't matter," Mallory said her arms turning to heavy strings of taffy. "He has an interest in you."

Austin tensed.

"Cool it, Hulk," Mallory said her eyes focused on Austin. "He has an interest but he says he doesn't. I know him so well, I can feel it. I don't want to be with him."

"We should keep going," Noah said lightly touching Austin's shoulder. Austin flinched and Noah stared into his eyes. "The sooner we get there, the sooner this can be over."

Austin shook his head and took a step away. "This will never be over."

He walked away from the group stopping just at the edge of the light. Austin was much too close to the shadows.

Noah started to go to him but I grabbed his arm to stop him. "Let me."

"Are you sure?" Noah asked.

"I'm sure. It'll be fine," I said.

I flicked a quick glance at Marty as I walked closer

to the darkness. He didn't even try to hide his nervousness about me going to the edge of the circle of light. I forced myself to look away before I stopped walking.

"Austin," I said softly from a foot back. "Please come back to the SUV."

"I just need a minute, okay?"

"Um," I stammered as I tried to think of something that could get him to come back. Or at least further back from the shadows. Maybe he hadn't realized just how close he was. Another step or two and the darkness would swallow him.

The creatures were out there and they weren't far from us. They were squealing with delight and it probably had to do with just how close they were to him.

"If you need space from me I understand," I said chewing on a hangnail I suddenly noticed. "But you're too close to the shadows."

Austin snorted and turned his back to the darkness. His eyes locked with mine. "I don't need space from you. I need space from him."

"We can just pretend he's not here," I said.

"Maybe you can, but I can't. I can't stop thinking about him putting his hands on you," Austin said.

I frowned. "Please stop thinking about it. I dealt with it. And that big bruise on his cheek seems to indicate that you dealt with it too."

"A little bruise isn't going to stop a guy like that," Austin said.

"Doesn't it matter to you, even a little, that I'm in love with you? I love you, not Bradley," I said feeling the warmth on my tongue as I said the words.

The moment wasn't at all how I'd imagined but it didn't matter, not even a little. I was completely and utterly in love with Austin. I didn't care about Bradley, or what he felt or any of it. All I wanted was for Austin to come back to the SUV and away from the darkness.

His eyes were glued to mine as if he were trying to comprehend what I'd said. It was like I'd given him a present and he was slowly unwrapping it, savoring every moment.

"I love you too," he said letting a smile grow on his face. He opened his mouth to say something more but he was gone. In a blink, he was gone into the shadows.

CHAPTER SIXTEEN

I ran to the edge of the light and flailed my arms around inside of the shadows trying to find him. Desperately trying to grab a hold of something.

"Austin!" I screamed.

A beam of light from my right cut through the darkness. Someone was coming and slicing through the shadows with the flashlight. I couldn't look away. I didn't have time to see who was there.

A pair of blue eyes about ten feet into the darkness looked in our direction. Clicking squeaks came out of its mouth as if it were trying to find something.

"There," I said grabbing the hand holding the flashlight and aiming it at the creature's eyes.

The creature wailed before its eyes disappeared and it stepped out of the beam of light.

"Austin?" I called again.

"I'm here," he replied but his voice was soft. Muffled.

I drew in a breath before yanking the flashlight from the hand beside me.

"Hey!" Noah said reaching back toward me but I moved out of the way and into the darkness.

My breaths were quick as I moved the light around in every direction. I swept the ground in front of me with the light but my hand was shaking and I shivered with fear.

"Where are you?" I asked my eyes welling up with tears. Had I imagined his voice? I couldn't lose him. Not now. Not ever.

Something moved in front of me and I gasped so sharply my breath lodged in my throat. It felt like I couldn't breathe as something grabbed me and dragged me back toward the lights from the SUV.

We poured out of the darkness, tumbling into the light, spitting up gravel around us as we fell to the ground. Austin was half on top of me looking down at me. The same amount of damp fear was pooled in his eyes that had been in mine.

"I'm here," Austin said.

I placed my hands on his cheeks looking him over with shaky breaths. Was he missing an arm? A leg? Was he with me in one piece?

My hands roamed over him making sure there

wasn't anything out of place.

"I'm fine," he said. "That thing knocked me to the ground. I was still, so still and it couldn't find me."

"Don't ever do that to me again," I said as a tear rolled down the side of my face.

"I won't," Austin said offering me a smile filled with an overwhelming amount of love. My heart swelled with relief and before I could say anything, he placed his lips on mine.

He didn't care who was there. He didn't care who was watching and neither did I.

Austin put everything he felt for me into that kiss and it turned my entire body to moldable clay. I was his. Always and forever. And there wasn't anyone that could change that.

If the moment hadn't been enough to convince Bradley how Austin and I felt about each other, nothing would. Not that it mattered of course.

Austin rolled off of me and got to his feet. He offered me his hand to help me up and I took it with a smile. It felt ceremonial the way we walked hand in hand back to the SUV.

Austin looked at me and grinned. "We're leaving. If you want to come with us to find the church, now is the time."

There was no vote. It was Austin making a decision he felt was the best for all of us and I believed he was right. We didn't need another night in the open. We needed a place to stay. A place we could be safe.

Of course, we didn't know if that place would be the church, but we didn't have time to sit around and wait. It was time to figure out how we were going to be safe with the evil that was out there.

We drove through the night, taking our time as we moved down the road. Marty checked the map on his phone whenever he could.

There had been a road sign six miles back indicating the nearest city. It seemed as though we were on track to make it by morning.

My nerves were making my fingers shake. What would they be like? What if it was some kind of trick?

"We should have some kind of plan," I said.

"A plan?" Marty asked.

I chewed my fingernail. "Just in case. What if it's some kind of trick?"

"Maybe I'll go first... alone," Austin said and I was shaking my head before he even finished his sentence. He glanced in my direction. "And if all goes well, I'll come back for you."

"What if all doesn't go well?" I asked.

Austin shrugged as if he hadn't thought that far ahead. "I'll be armed."

"There's probably not going to be anyone there anyway," Mallory mumbled from the furthest back seat. "It's only a matter of time before we're gone too. I'm not even sure why we bother."

"It isn't going to be like this forever," Noah said.

Mallory snorted. "What makes you so sure?"

Noah groaned and shook his head. "No one is making you fight for your life."

"Stop the car," Mallory said. I turned and looked into her fiery, wild eyes. Her hands gripped the back of the seat. "Let me out."

"I'm not stopping the car," Austin said. "Everyone needs to calm down."

"No one wants me here," Mallory said. Bradley kept his head down. "So, just let me go."

Austin slowed the car but he wasn't going to stop. He just wanted to drive safely with all the commotion going on.

"If I want to leave, you can't keep me against my will," Mallory said hitting the seats with her palms. "That's kidnapping."

"You're not a kid," Noah said. "Although, you are acting like one."

"Noah," Austin said in a rough voice. "Knock it off."

Tears streaked Mallory's face and my heart sank into my stomach. She hadn't deserved any of what had happened to her.

"Mallory," Austin said looking at her in the

rearview mirror. "I'm not letting you out. I don't want anything to happen to you."

"Like you care!" she spat.

"I care," Austin said.

I wanted to echo him but I feared that if I spoke it would only spark more anger.

"Well," Marty said in an oddly calm voice. He turned and there was a softness in his eyes. "I want you here."

Mallory opened her mouth, looking like she wanted to scream at him or maybe bite his head off like a wild animal. But she hesitated. She must have seen the same thing in his eyes that I had.

Marty was telling the truth. He didn't want her to leave.

She didn't say anything, but her hands relaxed. They slid off the seat as she leaned back.

Mallory's eyes stayed on Marty even when he turned to face forward. She turned to look out the window the second she caught me watching her.

"There's another road sign," Austin said. "See that on the map?"

"Hmm," Marty said studying his phone. "Yeah!" He cleared his throat and changed the tone of his voice to sound like the one used on his GPS app. "You should arrive at your destination in two hours."

I covered my chuckle. "You're making that up."

"I am but I think it's a pretty good guess," Marty said leaning forward to show me the phone.

I studied for a moment and nodded. His guess seemed like a fair one to me, which meant that we were going to have to figure out exactly what we were going to do when we got there.

Austin must have had the same thought. "When we get there, Lucy and I will go in and check it out first."

"What? No way," Marty said. "I'm coming too."

"No, no, no," I said shaking my head. "This makes the most sense."

"Are you kidding me? How does it make any sense?" Marty asked. "I don't want to lose you, Lucy. You're all I have left."

I drew in a breath through my nose. "And of course I don't want to lose you either, but I have to do what I think will keep you safe."

"Maybe I need to keep you safe," Marty said.

"Let's just all go together," Mallory said. "Strength in numbers, right?"

Silence filled the SUV. I was trying to find a way to argue with her but maybe she was right. Maybe we didn't need to separate, because together we were a team.

A crazy team where half of us didn't even like the other half, but still we were a team.

CHAPTER SEVENTEEN

The sun had been up for only minutes when we finally drove into the town where we'd find the church. My entire body felt like it was being touched by a low electric current. It was almost as though I could hear the buzzing in my ears.

Austin turned the lights off and carefully steered his way through the streets as Marty gave him directions as best as he could. The SUV was moving at an apprehensive crawl.

"There it is," Noah said leaning between the seats as he pointed at the steeple.

After a quick second, Noah leaned back onto his seat like a turtle going back into its shell. Austin must have felt a similar way because he slowed the SUV and pulled up to the curb two blocks away from the church.

The silence inside the SUV was palpable. We had arrived and I couldn't help but feel as though I was glued to my seat.

No one moved. There was a staleness in the air much like that of old corn chips.

I cracked open the door for a bit of fresh air and Mallory gasped as if she expected something terrible to happen.

"Well," I said pausing as I built my courage. "Are we ready?"

"I'm as ready as I'll ever be," Marty said.

"Who wants a gun?" Austin asked.

Mallory shook her head. "No, thanks."

The rest of us all nodded.

We stood at the back of the SUV as Austin passed out a gun to each of us. I tucked my gun into the back of my pants and covered it with my shirt. It wasn't like we wanted to scare or intimidate them, we only wanted to do what we needed to do to protect ourselves should it come to that.

The streets were empty. There weren't any sounds in the area but I couldn't shake the feeling that there were eyes on us.

It was a chilly morning. The light breeze whistled through the leaves and prickled the skin on my cheeks.

Austin closed the back of the SUV and locked the

doors. If we needed to leave, getting back to the car would be essential considering it had not only our supplies contained within it but also our life-saving lights.

The SUV was our heart. It was what kept us alive.

We walked down the road crossing at the sidewalk. Austin and I led the way. My eyes darted around the area so quickly it was giving me a sharp headache at my temples.

As we approached the church, a man exited, holding his arms out to both sides. There was a warm, welcoming smile stretched across his face.

"Good morning," he said as he studied each one of us. "It looks like you folks are in need of a place to stay. How have your travels been? By the looks of it, I say rough."

He lowered his eyes and hands as he offered us a sympathetic frown.

"That would be putting it mildly," Mallory muttered not nearly loud enough for the man to hear.

"Please, come in, come in," the man said before holding up his index finger. "Oh, I almost forgot." He stretched out his hand toward Austin, likely because he was the closest. "I'm Lucas. I run things around here."

"Austin," he said shaking Lucas's hand.

Lucas turned to me. "And you are?"

"Lucy and this is my brother Marty," I said shaking his hand.

His grip was firm but soft and his eyes were filled with a cheer I hadn't seen since before the creatures had appeared. I'd thought they'd wiped every bit of cheer that had been left off of the planet when they came to the surface. Though, it wasn't like I had even seen it a lot even before the creatures.

The others introduced themselves and he gave them all equally welcoming smiles. It had softened the entire group so much so that the tension we'd carried with us blew away in the breeze.

"You'll be safe here," Lucas said as we walked up a set of wide stairs to the tall church doors. "There are only twelve of us here at the moment but we hope others will see our messages soon. Your arrival gives us hope. It proves that we were right that there are others out there who have survived this horrible, horrible attack on humanity." He shook his head as he lowered his gaze. "Just awful."

"How do you keep the creatures away?" Austin asked as he opened the door. The rusted hinges squeaked in a pitch similar to the sounds the creatures made.

Lucas raised his brows and pointed up to the corners of the building. "Lights. Lots and lots of lights.

And by the looks of the SUV you parked down the road, you all have figured out how to keep them away as well."

He'd been watching us. They'd probably seen us coming from miles away peering out from the top of the steeple. Did that mean he also knew we were armed? Something told me that he did.

We walked into the church and my nose was accosted by the smell of frankincense. It wasn't fresh, but the walls and carpeting had seemed to have been stained with the intense aroma.

The scent was dizzying. If Lucas noticed it, he didn't mention it. His nose probably had been quite accustomed to the scent while it made my stomach feel hollow.

There were a set of stairs in the middle of the entranceway that let upward and another set on the left and right that were much smaller leading downward. Lucas gestured to the middle set and continued to lead the way.

At the top was a small table with a stack of thin booklets. There was a black and white picture of the church printed on the cover.

We followed Lucas through a wide opening into a smaller room. There was a wooden podium and an elaborate statue of a man in robes looking down at us with praying hands.

Stretched out in front of us, was a short aisle that led to the front of the church. There were pews on each side and at the front, several people were seated casually, whispering as they cast frequent glances in our direction.

"It's amazing that all four walls are still standing, isn't it?" Lucas said glancing at us, his hands pressed together at the palms resting lightly against his lower chest, just like the statue had been.

There was a calmness and peacefulness that radiated out from Lucas. But it wasn't quite enough to calm me.

"Yeah, sure is," Noah said.

The inside of the church felt a bit too dark. The pale blues and yellows of the stained glass windows didn't allow enough sunlight into the room.

"How do you keep them from digging up through the basement?" I asked and everyone turned to look at me. Everyone.

"We've discovered there is a certain pitch they aren't particularly fond of," Lucas said.

I remembered when Mallory had screamed in the trees and the young creatures hadn't seemed to like it.

"We play it at night," a guy said as he popped up out of the front pew. He ran his hand through his wild, slightly curly blonde hair that was in desperate need of a trim. "I'm Samuel."

"My son," Lucas added proudly.

Samuel stood next to his father with his arms crossed. They could have been twins except for that Samuel was significantly taller.

Lucas introduced us to the other four people sitting in the pews. They smiled at us politely but their names fluttered like butterflies from my mind just as quickly as they had entered it.

"The others are out gathering supplies from the town," Lucas said.

Samuel nodded. "We typically take turns."

"They'll be back and forth several times before dinnertime, you can meet them then," Lucas said with a grin that nearly closed his eyes. "They probably saw you when you came into town though. We keep a pretty close eye on everything."

Samuel looked at me, cocking his head to the side slightly. "You are all welcome to stay as long as you like. We have more than enough supplies and tons of space."

"We even have a nice place for you to park your car so that you don't have to worry about it getting stolen," Lucas said.

"That happens?" Austin asked trying to conceal the worry in his eyes. "Things get stolen?"

Lucas shrugged and gave us a gentle frown. "From

time to time things go missing. Not often but it has happened."

"Just people passing through, we think," Samuel said. "We have signs up to come here for help but I think people are wary."

"Yes," Lucas said. "They think it's a trap."

It seemed as though we'd be safe from the creatures based on the condition of the building, but it was hard to feel comfortable in the space with the strangers surrounding us. I was struggling to hide my apprehension about staying.

"Would you like to see where you'd be staying before you decide?" Samuel asked leaning slightly closer.

He smelled of spicy soap and cologne. Clean. I wanted to pour a bottle of perfume over my entire body.

I glanced over at Austin and then at Marty to see if I could decipher their thoughts based on their expression.

"Sure," Marty said answering for us.

"You guys don't need to look so scared," Samuel said with a slight smirk that looked like it was on the verge of turning into a laugh. "We're just normal people."

"It's just strange to be around people again," Austin said as if that would explain.

Samuel's head bobbed up and down as if he understood. "I can imagine. You don't need to commit to anything and for the most part, you're free to come and go during the day as you please. Let's just take a look, all right? No harm in looking."

CHAPTER EIGHTEEN

As we followed Samuel down the aisle, Lucas whispered to the group of people. I could feel their eyes on our backs as we walked away.

"What was it like outside of the city?" Samuel asked as we turned the corner and took one of the smaller sets of stairs into the basement.

"Quiet during the day and scary as hell during the night," Noah said.

Samuel rubbed his hands together. "Then this is going to be a real treat for you."

"You're not scared at night?" I asked.

"Maybe a little," Samuel admitted. "But not much."

"Do you sleep during the day?" Mallory asked.

Samuel tossed her an awkward glance. "No. Should we?"

"That's what we've been doing," Mallory said.

Samuel widened his eyes at her as he led us through a small cafeteria. "Well, you don't have to do that here. Unless you want to, of course."

"I hate sleeping during the day. It's nearly impossible," Mallory said batting her eyelashes at Samuel. Bradley groaned and rolled his eyes.

He narrowed his eyes at her. "Something in your eye?"

"What?" Mallory said touching the corner of her eye. "Oh, no. I'm fine, thanks."

Her cheeks were the color of a dozen red roses. She looked from side to side nervously as she rubbed the side of her face.

"This way," Samuel said pointing as he led us down a short hallway with several rooms each with a number on the door. "These used to be classrooms but we turned them into sleeping quarters."

He turned the knob and opened the last door on the right. The concrete walls were painted with a pale shade of light blue that reminded me of where I went to grade school. There were ten air mattresses lined up in the room.

"We thought there would be more people coming," Samuel explained as if he knew my unasked question. "You guys can have this room to yourselves for now."

"How many rooms are there?" I asked.

"Five on this side, five on the other and my dad sleeps upstairs," Samuel said smiling at me.

Mallory stepped forward breaking Samuel's gaze that was locked onto me. "So, if you have the space, can I have my own room?"

"Um," Samuel stammered as he looked at each of us. "I guess that would be fine. I just assumed you'd all want to stay together."

I was tempted to request a room that wouldn't include Bradley but the look on his face me keep my mouth closed. It looked as though he was upset enough about having ruined whatever he and Mallory had together.

Bradley was someone that always wanted what he didn't have. And now he was probably regretting it in a world where he didn't have anyone.

"I prefer my own space," Mallory said shooting a sharp look at Bradley.

"Okay, well, follow me then," Samuel said. They walked out of the doorway leaving it open. I exhaled but it got stuck in my throat when he stepped back into the opening. "By the way, we'll have dinner in the cafeteria at five. Don't be late."

He was smiling but I didn't think the time he'd given was merely a suggestion. It seemed more like it was a requirement.

He disappeared like a magician without the cloud

of smoke but it didn't feel like he was gone. My eyes moved around the room hesitating in each corner as if I was expecting to find a little camera.

There wasn't anything there, but it still felt like we were being watched. But maybe it was just because we were in a church.

Mallory's words floated through the doorway but they were indecipherable mumbles. Her giggles, however, were as clear as a bright summer day.

"So, I guess we broke up," Bradley said plopping down on one of the air mattresses. "Not that any of you care, of course."

"It was kind of obvious," Marty said. "And Mallory already told us."

"Can't say you didn't deserve it," Noah added.

Bradley's shoulders slumped. "Kick a man when he's down why don't you?"

Noah shrugged. I wanted nothing more than to change the subject as soon as possible. Even though it wasn't my fault, I couldn't help but feel connected to the break-up.

Maybe at some point, I'd have to talk to Mallory but that day wasn't today. And I was pretty sure it wasn't going to be tomorrow either.

Maybe she and Samuel would fall in love and then it wouldn't matter. Mallory wanted to be with some-one, that much I could tell. She wasn't someone that liked to be alone. Perhaps she didn't even know how to be alone.

Austin and I locked eyes. His expression remained neutral and it worried me that I couldn't tell what he was thinking.

I could read Bradley's expressions like a book, but with Austin it was different. He hid what he was thinking and feeling. Austin was more of a mystery.

"Do we have to stay in here until dinner?" Marty asked. "Kind of feels like a jail cell."

"It's bigger than the SUV," Noah said lowering himself down on one of the mattresses. He pulled his cap down over his eyes and crossed his arms as he leaned back on the pillow. "And significantly more comfortable."

Samuel hadn't stayed in the room with Mallory long. I could hear his footsteps getting softer as he made his way back down the short hallway.

"You might as well get some rest," Austin said gesturing at the air mattress behind me.

"What about you?" I asked.

He shook his head. "I'll wait. I think we should probably take turns."

"Is that really necessary?" Noah asked mumbling his words. "You saw the condition of the building. You saw the people living here. Whatever they're doing is working."

"Plus it's daytime," Marty added.

"Yeah but we're inside, and if the lights go out, it'll be pitch black," Austin said.

Noah chuckled. "If the lights go out, there isn't anything you can do to help us if you're awake. Might be better if you sleep through everything if that happens."

Austin shifted his weight back and forth several times before settling into a wide stance. He glanced at me as he scratched the back of his bicep.

"I guess you're right," Austin said lowering himself down to the bed next to mine.

I wanted to curl up with Austin but for some reason, I didn't. The door was open, our brothers were in the room, and Bradley was there with us. It wasn't like I wanted to kick Bradley when he was down and rub my relationship with Austin in his face even if being next to him would have helped me sleep better.

We gave the people in the church our trust, whether or not it was a smart thing to do. Exhaustion had control over our decisions. I hadn't even tried to fight it... I fell asleep.

It hadn't felt like it had been a long rest when I woke to someone gently shaking me. Austin was looking into my eyes with a bright smile on his fast. There were still bags under his eyes, but I could tell he'd gotten some sleep.

"It's time to get some food," Austin said.

I frowned. My eyelids felt like they were being pulled back down. The sleep although short had been fantastic. My entire body was relaxed and I wanted more. I needed more.

"Come on, lazy bones," Austin said pulling on my hand.

I groaned but I let him pull me to my feet. The room was empty except for Austin and me.

"Did the others go to the cafeteria?" I asked.

My question alone was enough to cause Austin to hesitate. He turned and wrapped his arms around my waist.

"We're all alone," Austin said in a deep voice that vibrated my insides. "We could close the door. Skip dinner and spend a little time together."

I leaned into him. "That sounds amazing but we can't do that. They're all out there waiting for us. And this is a church... pretty sure that's breaking a law of some kind."

"There's no law against that," Austin said laughing as he pulled me closer. I could feel just how badly he would have liked to stay in the room with me.

But we couldn't... could we?

Austin's hands moved down my back, curving around my bottom. I wrapped my arms around his neck and melted into him.

I sighed as he leaned in, his eyes glowing orange with excitement. His lips glided against mine and my knees weakened as the electric heat surged through my veins.

I wanted nothing more than to close the door and push him down on the bed. But the plates and silverware clink-clanking down the hall forced me to take a step back.

"We should go before they come looking for us," I said without letting go of his hand as I led us toward the door and into the hall.

Austin noisily dragged his feet but stumbled along behind me. As we stepped inside the cafeteria, everyone looked up at us. They were all sitting there with their plates in front of them.

"Just made it," Samuel said smacking Austin on the back. "Go on and fill up your plates. Join us. My dad was just about to say Grace."

"Right, sorry," Austin said. "We're all so tired... it was hard to open my eyes."

"I can imagine," Samuel said watching us as we scooped canned green beans, instant potatoes, and grilled canned meat onto our plates.

We sat down at the end of the table across from each other. Lucas stood and folded his hands, he bowed his head slightly as he began to thank God for our food.

Everyone ate in near silence. There were a few whispers complementing the woman, Bev, who had prepared the meal.

At the end of the meal, Lucas came and stood at the end of the table. He looked back and forth between Austin and me.

"I'd like to show you what we do to prepare for night time," Lucas said keeping his gaze planted on Austin.

"Um, sure," Austin said picking up his plate.

Lucas held up his palm before waving his hand at Bev. "They'll take care that."

"Oh, it's not a problem," Austin said.

"Really, they'll clean up. We don't have a lot of time," Lucas said as Bev reached around Austin and grabbed his plate.

"It's no problem, sir," the short, gray-haired woman said bowing several times as she walked away from the table.

Lucas turned to me, holding my gaze for a long moment. "You and Mallory should go along with Bev."

"What?" I asked letting my mouth drop open slightly.

"She could use your help. Do you have a problem with that?" Lucas asked.

"No, I guess not," I said even though I kind of did. It felt like I was being left behind to do kitchen work just because I was a woman. But maybe it didn't have anything to do with my gender.

Bev waddled up next to me and gestured at my plate. "Come with me, okay?"

I nodded as Mallory walked over to us with her arms crossed. "Guess I'm here to help."

Over my shoulder, I watched as Lucas and Samuel led Austin, Noah, Marty, and Bradley up the stairs. I let out my frustration from between my lips and smiled at Bev. Everyone else had left so it would be just the three of us.

Bev led us into the kitchen glancing back at us as if she were afraid we might just disappear. "No one likes cleaning."

"Everyone should learn to clean their own plates," I muttered.

Bev looked at me as if I'd said the most horrible thing she's ever heard. "It's not hard. I'll show you."

I bit back my heavy sigh. What did Bev think of me? It didn't matter, at least that's what I told myself as I watched her show me a skill I've known since I was seven. How to wash my own plate.

CHAPTER NINETEEN

Mallory went off to her own room without saying anything to me. There was no doubt that she hated me just as much as she hated Bradley.

I could have told her that I had nothing to do with it, but I would have been wasting my breath. She wouldn't have cared. She wouldn't have listened. Mallory's mind had been made up and I was the enemy.

It had been at least an hour before Austin and the others returned. I wished I would have been able to sleep, but my mind wouldn't allow it. I sat up abruptly as they entered the room all wearing smiles.

"Where were you?" I asked.

Austin sat down on the mattress next to me. "Samuel and Lucas showed us around."

"You should see the lights," Marty said.

"I wish I could have but I had to stay with Bev and learn how to wash dishes," I said clenching my hands.

Austin leaned back and wrapped his arm around my shoulder. "They wanted us to know where every-thing was located just in case something should happen."

"That makes sense," I said with a groan. "And when disaster strikes, I'll make sure all the dishes are sparkling."

"He probably just thought you didn't have any interest in any of it," Marty said.

I shrugged and snuggled up closer to Austin. Being in his arms helped me feel better. It wasn't like Austin couldn't just tell me where everything was and what their routine was like.

"So we're just trapped down here during the night?" I asked. "What are we supposed to do?"

"Sleep," Marty said.

Noah was already pulling his cap down over his eyes. "He said we're safe to turn out the lights if we want."

"Oh, they do have one rule though," Austin said pressing his cheek to the side of my head.

"Really? Just one rule? Something tells me there are a lot of secret rules here," I said exhaling out the last of my frustration and letting tiredness re-enter my body. "Well? What's the rule?"

"When it's dark, we need to keep quiet," Austin said. "No talking."

Noah's mouth stretching into a wide yawn. "Yeah, and we're breaking that rule right now."

"Shut up," Austin said throwing a pillow at him.

Noah took the pillow and covered his head with it.

"Thought you could sleep anywhere?" I teased.

"I can," Noah grumbled. "But it's easier when it's quiet."

"What time do you think it is anyway?" I turned to face Austin with my nose scrunched up.

Austin looked at the invisible watch on his wrist and shook his head. "Not sure exactly but I bet it's still early. Before eight?"

I yawned but I wasn't sure I could sleep knowing it was dark outside. If there were creatures around us, I couldn't hear them. If they were digging tunnels below us, it didn't disturb the ground.

It felt safe inside the church but I didn't know if we actually were. For all we knew, everyone inside had just been lucky. We'd been fortunate in our home for a long time before the creatures decided to tunnel into our basement.

"Want to take turns sleeping?" Austin asked. He must have noticed the concern that felt like it was oozing out of my every pore.

"Do you think we should?" I asked wanting his honest opinion.

I followed Austin's gaze as he looked around the room. Bradley was lying on his side with his back to us, Marty's eyes were closed but his breathing was much too quick, and Noah was either asleep or almost there.

"Maybe just to be safe," Austin said. "I feel like we should keep the lights on."

"I agree," I said.

"Rock, paper, scissors to see who sleeps first?" Austin asked.

I shrugged. "You should probably just get some rest. It looks like you need it."

"Ouch," he said placing his hand on his chest as if I'd hurt his feelings.

I bumped him lightly with my elbow. "You know that's not what I meant."

"I know," he whispered softly into my ear.

"Your eyes are bloodshot, that's all," I explained.

"It's not from tiredness, it's from the incense smoke upstairs," Austin said and I wasn't sure if he was joking or not.

I grinned. "Go on, get some rest. I'll wake you soon."

"How will you keep your eyes open?" Austin asked.

"I'll manage," I said. "I've been doing it for a while now. Nothing has changed except for our location."

Out of the corner of my eye, I noticed a shadow move into the doorway. Samuel cleared his throat as he pressed his hands against the insides of the frame and let his body swing forward slightly.

"I just wanted to make sure you were all settled," Samuel said.

Austin sat up straighter. "Thanks, yes."

"Good," Samuel said cocking his head to the side. "Is there something wrong with your bed?"

"No, no," Austin said shifting away slightly, clearly uncomfortable.

My cheeks felt impossibly hot. "Sorry, we were just wondering what time it was."

"Yeah, no clocks. We lost track of time a while back," Samuel said. "We just go by the sun."

"But you can't see the sun down here," I said narrowing my eyes slightly.

Samuel stared at me but ignored my comment. "Would you like the lights out now?"

"No," I said shaking my head. "We feel more comfortable with them on."

"If you insist," Samuel said. "It's easier to sleep with them off."

"Not for us," Austin said. "We've been sleeping during the day since the creatures arrived."

Samuel nodded. "You'll get used to it with time." He gestured to the air mattress next to mine. "Why don't you go to your own bed now and get some rest. If you're up for it, maybe you can go on a run with me in the morning."

"Um," Austin said glancing at me. "Maybe."

"It's a breeze. You'll see," Samuel said hitting the door frame with his knuckles. "Well, have a good night. See you for breakfast?"

"Of course," Austin answered but it felt more like Samuel had been asking me the way he had his eyes glued to me.

The others grumbled their responses only because they were half asleep not because they were ungrateful. Hopefully, Samuel had realized that.

Samuel disappeared from the doorway and turned off a light down the hall. It suddenly felt as though we were surrounded by darkness, but that was because we were.

As long as the lights stayed on outside and the sounds the creatures didn't like continued to play I had to hope that we'd make it until morning.

"Good night," Austin said placing a kiss on my forehead.

I grabbed his collar and pulled him back for a second before he could get away.

"It seems I'm required to sleep in my own bed," Austin said as if explaining why he was leaving.

It had been painfully clear that sharing wasn't going to be allowed, not that anything would have happened with our brothers across the room. It just would have been nice to be near him.

I sighed. "Good night."

"I love you," Austin said into my ear.

I bit my lip wanting him to stay in my bed even more. "I love you too."

And with that, Austin crawled onto the air mattress and laid on his side. He stared at me for a moment but his eyelids became heavy. His lips were curled upward as he drifted off to a dreamland I hoped was altogether creature free.

CHAPTER TWENTY

Something was tapping my shoulder but it sounded like metal clinking and clanking together. My eyes opened and latched onto Marty who was standing next to me, tapping me at a steady beat.

I sat up and my ears registered the noises coming down the hall from the kitchen. Either Bev was preparing breakfast or I had missed it.

"Oatmeal," Marty said sticking out his tongue. "Made with water."

Marty hadn't ever liked oatmeal. He could have added six tablespoons of sugar and it would have still made him gag.

When he'd been six or seven years old, he'd thrown up peaches and cream oatmeal and ever since then he hadn't been able to stomach any oatmeal. I understood because I felt the same way about hot dogs.

"We still have the supplies in the SUV," I said. "You should go help yourself to what's in there before they move it to the safe garage or whatever."

"Austin's going to do that?" Marty asked.

"Yeah, I think so but I'm not sure. Why? Shouldn't he?"

Marty shrugged. "So, we're staying here then?"

"I think so," I said squeezing my eyebrows together. "It's not like we have a lot of options. Do you not like it here?"

"I don't know. It just kind of gives me the creeps," Marty said looking around the room as though checking to make sure the room wasn't bugged.

I nodded. It was almost like I didn't want to respond verbally in case it was.

"Well, if you have a better idea I'm all ears," I said stretching my arms over my head as I sat up in the bed.

"I wish I did. I'll work on one," Marty said jerking his head to the side. "Come on, they're waiting. They seem," he lowered his voice, "impatient."

Breakfast was quiet but it was filling. My stomach hadn't been that satisfied since my mom had been the one to prepare the meals.

Bev asked Mallory and me if we'd be willing to help out again. She said it had gone so much quicker than when she has to do everything on her own.

I helped with a smile. Mallory helped but gritted her teeth the entire time.

Samuel and Lucas took Marty, Noah, and Austin out on a run. Bradley had declined, saying he didn't feel well.

Every minute they were gone was agony. I couldn't stop thinking about what I'd do if they didn't return. If I'd be stuck with Bradley and Mallory, it would be worse than being eaten by a creature, at least it sure felt that way.

When we finished in the kitchen, I went back to the room. I wanted to sleep a little longer while it was daylight because I didn't get enough sleep taking shifts with Austin during.

Bradley was lying there on his side with his legs curled up to his chest. He didn't look well.

His eyes were closed and I was pretty sure he had no idea I was even in the room. I looked around as if checking to make sure no one was watching before I placed my hand on his forehead.

"Holy shit," I said pulling my hand away to cover my mouth. Pretty sure I wasn't allowed to curse in a church.

Bradley was on fire.

I stood and leaned back against the wall. I didn't know what to do to help him but I couldn't just sit there and do nothing.

He'd been fine. It was like night and day how quickly he'd gotten sick. At least it had seemed that way.

Since his break up with Mallory, he hadn't said much.

"Bradley," I said as I shook his shoulders. "Wake up!"

He groaned as he tried to open his eyes. "What?"

"You're burning up."

"Yeah, I don't feel so good," he said with a long moan. "Think it's something I ate."

"How long have you felt this way?" I asked.

His head rolled to the side and he mumbled something I couldn't make out.

"Bradley! How long have you felt sick?" I asked.

"Not long. Started yesterday after we ate I guess," he said. "I just need rest."

I glanced toward the door wondering if I should talk to Mallory about it. Although I was likely the last person she wanted to talk to about anything including Bradley.

There was always Lucas. He was running the place, he'd probably had a suggestion or maybe they even had medicine that could help.

It felt like I was stuck between a rock and a hard place. I could talk to Mallory, Lucas, or do nothing.

Maybe Bradley was right. Perhaps all he needed was rest.

I looked down at him. His hair was slicked loosely to the side with dampness.

A long sigh escaped from between my lips as I pushed myself away from the wall and toward the door. The only thing I was sure of was that I couldn't do nothing.

CHAPTER TWENTY-ONE

I stepped into the church squinting at the amount of bright light coming in through the stained glass windows. Although there was light downstairs, it hadn't quite been the same.

I stopped at the back of the church. Lucas wasn't there, but a small group of women, including Bev, was.

One of them stared at me before whispering something to the others. I turned but I didn't make it far before someone placed a hand on my shoulder.

"Can I help you with something?" a tall woman with round glasses asked. I couldn't for the life of me remember her name.

"I'm looking for Lucas," I said biting my cheek. His name tasted salty on my tongue.

"He's out with the others," the woman said. She cocked her head slightly and narrowed her eyes. "I'm in charge while he's out. It's Lucy, right? Do you need something? You look troubled."

I grabbed my elbow. "Do you have any medicine here?"

"What kind of medicine are you looking for?"

I bit my cheek. "Fever reducer."

"Oh, no, dear! Are you sick?" The woman reached her hand forward and slapped it to my forehead.

"Not me," I said shaking my head. "My friend."

"Oh," she said letting her hand fall away. "Take me to him."

I turned and started down the stairs but I stopped. "How did you know it was Bradley?"

"Sorry?" she said her forehead creasing.

"You said take me to him. How did you know it wasn't Mallory that was sick?" I asked.

She stared blankly and then gestured for me to continue. "Because she's not in the same room as you. I talked with Lucas a bit and it seems as though she wanted her own space so I just assumed it must have been Bradley that was ill."

"Oh," I said. "You're very good with names."

The woman beamed. "I used to be a teacher. In the school across the street in fact. I had to be good with names."

"I'm terrible at them," I said. "Although I didn't really realize it until just recently."

The woman laughed. "Does that mean you don't remember my name?"

"Sorry," I said.

"It's Laurie," she said still smiling. "So, what's going on with your friend."

"He's lethargic and has a fever," I said.

"Hmm," Laurie said slowing her stride as we neared the room. "Maybe you should wait out here, dear."

I nodded even though I wasn't sure why it was necessary. Laurie entered the room and stared at him with her arms crossed. After a long moment, she offered me a thin-lipped smile and closed the door.

Hinges squeaked behind me and I turned sharply. Mallory was standing there staring at the closed door.

"What's going on?" she asked softly.

"Bradley's sick," I said keeping all emotion out of my voice and refusing to look at her.

She stepped out of the room with her arms crossed.

"Is he okay?" she asked with a softness to her voice. It was clear she still cared deeply for him.

"I don't know," I said. "He was sweating a lot. Really lethargic. I think he had a really high fever."

"Oh," she said. After a moment she sighed. "I know it wasn't your fault.

"What wasn't my fault?"

She looked at me blinking several times. "It wasn't

the first time Bradley hit on someone else while we were together."

"Why did you put up with it?" I asked.

"There wasn't anyone left. I figured it was finally over," Mallory said. "I know he never loved me but I thought maybe he could."

I felt sad for her even though I was almost positive that hadn't been her intention. Mallory was gorgeous but her self esteem seemed to be nonexistent.

"Anyway," she said shaking her head. "It doesn't matter now."

"I don't have an interest in Bradley that way," I blurted even though it seemed like she hadn't wanted to continue the conversation. "Yes we'd been a couple but he cheated. I'm over him."

"I know," Mallory said.

The door opened and Laurie stepped into the hall, closing the door behind her with a click that echoed in the hallway. She looked back and forth between Mallory and me with a sadness in her eyes.

"I'm sorry, he seems quite sick," Laurie said. "I'm going to get him some water but I don't really think there is much we can do but to wait for him to fight whatever it is off."

"So you don't have any medicine?" I asked.

"Not that will help him," Laurie said lowering her head. "Excuse me."

She turned and dashed down the hallway. Moments later she returned carrying a tall plastic water bottle with a bent straw poking out of the top.

Laurie didn't say anything as she slipped back into the room.

"Can we see him?" Mallory asked after Laurie had closed the door. "Although I'm probably the last person he wants to see."

"I don't know." I shrugged.

"I'm worried about him," she said.

"It's probably just a bug. He'll be fine," I said offering her a reassuring smile.

Mallory nodded. "Just seems so sudden. I usually can feel it coming on but he hadn't mentioned anything."

"He hadn't been talking much lately," I reminded her.

Several minutes passed before either of us spoke. Mallory took several steps forward and placed her hand on the wall next to the door.

"I want to see him," she said frowning. "Why does it feel like we're not allowed to go inside?"

I shook my head but felt relieved it wasn't just me feeling that way.

My thoughts were disrupted when the front doors of the church banged open loudly. Feet pounded aggressively as someone came down the stairs. It wasn't long before a wide-eyed Lucas came into view.

"I heard about Bradley. How is he?" Lucas asked as he slowed his pace.

"We don't know," I said shaking my head. "Laurie is in there with him."

His head bobbed slowly. "Good. She's an excellent care-taker."

"How did you hear he wasn't feeling well?" I asked unable to stop my eyes from narrowing.

Lucas pointed at a two-way radio strapped to his hip. "Laurie messaged me. I came back as soon as I could."

"Can you help him?" Mallory asked.

"I'll do what I can," Lucas said with an impossibly small smile. "Never underestimate the power of prayer."

Lucas opened the door and disappeared inside the room. I could hear them whispering but I couldn't make out a single word.

"How can it be so bad that he needs to be saved by prayer?" Mallory asked. "What is going on here?"

"I don't know," I said as I turned to see Marty, Austin, and Noah coming our way.

Austin stepped up to the door and looked over his shoulder at me. "Is it bad?"

"We don't know what's going on," I said. "They have the door closed."

"They won't allow you in?" Austin asked his brow wrinkled with confusion.

I shrugged. "I don't know. We didn't ask."

"Well, I'm going in," Austin said reaching out toward the doorknob.

He turned it but didn't get the door open more than a few inches before Lucas stepped into the small opening and stopped the door from going any wider.

"I'm sorry to inform you that things are not good," Lucas said.

"What's going on?" Austin asked.

"We're doing what we can, but he's vomiting, convulsing... we can't even get him to talk to us anymore," Lucas said in a quiet voice.

"Can we see him?" Mallory asked.

Lucas shook his head. "I'm not sure it's a good idea. "We're going to need to quarantine this room."

"I don't understand," I said wrapping my arms around my middle. "How could this have happened? He was fine before we came here."

Lucas glared at me. It was clear he was taking offense to my words.

Lucas took the radio from his belt and noisy static cut through the air. He kept his eyes on mine as he pressed a button.

"Samuel," Lucas said hesitating for a response.

"I'm here," Samuel said his voice fuzzy as it came back through the radio.

"Need your help downstairs."

"On my way," Samuel replied.

Lucas slipped the radio back onto his belt. "We'll get you all set up in a new room in no time."

"Please," Mallory begged. "Let me see him. Maybe there is something I can do to help."

Lucas looked over his shoulder into the room. Laurie began whimpering loudly.

"He didn't make it," Laurie said.

A shiver ran down my spine. I looked at Austin as my hand began to shake.

"What?" I asked as if she'd spoken in another language. "That can't be."

Mallory dropped to her knees and pressed her hands to her face. She released a wail that would have scared the creatures away had they been near.

Marty knelt down next to Mallory and did his best to comfort her.

"We are so incredibly sorry for your loss," Lucas said bowing his head. "We can discuss plans for a service when you're ready."

"I don't understand," I mumbled.

It felt like my head was floating away from my

body. Everything was moving too quickly. Nothing made any sense.

I was waiting for someone to wake me and tell me it was all a horrible dream. Before I knew it, we were being ushered into another room.

Samuel was telling us he was sorry for our loss and that if anyone should need anything, anything at all, not to hesitate to ask him. They had medicine to help us sleep. But why didn't they had anything that could have helped Bradley?

The tears that rolled down my cheeks were little coals as I stared at Samuel's moving lips. Nothing he said made any sense. But he hadn't stayed long. Moments later, he closed the door and the room began to spin like I was on a merry-go-round.

CHAPTER TWENTY-TWO

I had no idea what time it was but I could hear someone moving around in the hallway. Austin was in a seated position with his head back against the wall, but his eyes were closed. He must have tried to stay awake but there is only so much a single person can do before you can't fight off sleep any longer.

The light was on in our room. Mallory was curled up into a small ball on the air mattress in the corner of the room. I moved silently to the door, not wanting to wake her.

I pressed my ear to the door and listened. It was a long while before they started moving again.

Someone complained about how heavy Bradley was. Another person shushed them.

Their feet scratched the floor as they moved by the room. They tried to be quiet but they were failing.

It had felt like minutes had gone by before I didn't hear anything. I looked at the others over my shoulder before turning the knob and looking out into the hallway to make sure the coast was clear.

The only thing in the hallway was the dim light flowing from the lights they'd left on in the kitchen. It felt cold as I stepped out into the hall and glanced over toward the room Bradley had been in.

The door was open and the light was on but there weren't any sounds coming from the room. I wasn't sure why but my feet were leading me closer.

My breathing was shallow as I leaned into the room and looked toward the mattress Bradley had been on. Nothing had looked peculiar except for the fact that the bed was empty. It was hard to believe Bradley was really gone after all I hadn't seen him.

The cup of water Laurie had brought for Bradley was tipped over at the side of the bed surrounded by a small pool of water. I walked over to pick up the cup wondering if he'd been able to drink any of it.

As I picked up the cup, I noticed some white residue that was lightly coating the floor. I reached out my finger to touch it but stopped myself. I moved it around with the tip of my shoe noticing its damp but somewhat flaky consistency.

I pulled the top off the cup and noticed the same residue clinging to the side. Why would they have given Bradley water inside a cup that had been so dirty? The residue wasn't like a hard water stain but I didn't know what else it could have been. It couldn't have been medicine since they said they didn't have anything that could have helped him.

Where had they taken him anyway? My knees felt weak as I walked down the hall and into the kitchen. I set the cup down next to the sink and chewed my fingernail for a moment.

I wanted to see Bradley.

I needed to see him for closure. He may have been a thorn in my side but I hadn't wanted him to die and especially not like this. Not with strangers at his side giving him dirty water to drink.

I went up the stairs and into the church. There were candles lit at the windows casting dancing shadows on the wall. It made the church feel far from safe.

I crossed my arms as a chill wiggled up and down my spine like a worm digging its way into the earth. Where was everyone? Sleeping?

I started making my way back out of the church when I heard voices. The words were indecipherable but it sounded like someone was scolding someone else. Lucas?

I walked quickly to the door at the front of the church and opened it slightly to make sure the lights were on. The entire neighborhood was glowing in the bright pale yellow color from the copious amounts of lights positioned perfectly around the roof.

Even though I still had my gun tucked into the back of my pants, I stepped out into the night with my nerves buzzing. A gun wouldn't stop the creatures if they came on me at once.

Why was I even thinking about my gun? I probably should have told someone where I was going.

I walked out around the side of the building where I'd heard the voices. Lucas, Samuel, and six others were standing shoulder to shoulder staring at something on the ground.

My feet stopped moving and I stepped closer to the building. I wasn't sure why but I didn't want to be seen.

Samuel looked at his father and nodded before lifting an axe over his head. What were they....

"Oh, God." The words slipped out of my mouth in a single gasping breath that tightened my throat.

Samuel lifted the axe again, letting it fall back toward the ground with as much force as he could put behind it. Something rolled away from his feet.

It wasn't until the fingers uncurled like a blooming flower that I realized what I was seeing. Bradley's arm.

They'd chopped it off. Like a butcher slaughtering cattle.

Bile stirred up the back of my throat and I had to swallow it back down. If they heard me vomit, my body might end up on the ground next to Bradley's.

I couldn't watch. Every time Samuel raised the axe, I gagged covering my ears as I looked away.

Finally, he stopped lifting the axe. There was so much light that when they stepped away, I could see the large hunks of Bradley split up on the ground.

Icy tears streamed down my face. I didn't know what to do. I felt helpless. All I could do was stand there in shock as each one of them picked up a piece and threw it into the darkness.

It was like they were making an offering. Their lips moved as if they were reciting something before throwing Bradley to the creatures.

I could hear them moving about... making their squealing noises. They were enjoying their feast.

"They're pleased!" Lucas said quietly but it had been loud enough that I could hear it. "Let's go."

I turned quickly, moving soundlessly as I made my way back inside the church.

My heart was pounding against my chest. The hard thumping was making it difficult to take in oxygen.

It felt like I was moving in slow motion as I skipped down the stairs and jogged through the cafeteria.

As I stepped in front of the door, reaching out for

the doorknob the door opened. I stumbled backward into the wall flailing my arms as though I was trying to find a breath to pull into my body.

"Lucy!" Austin said reaching out to me. His eyes were wide as he stared at me. "What are you doing out there?"

His eyes darted to his left as the doors to the church squeaked open and echoed through the basement. The stretched expression on his face indicated that he realized something was wrong.

Austin picked me up and dragged me back into the room. He wrapped his arms around me and I couldn't stop myself from silently sobbing and shaking.

"What's going on?" he whispered. "I was about to lose my shit. I woke up and you were gone."

"Something bad," I said my voice squeaking out between my lips. "We have to get out of here."

"I don't understand," Austin said shaking his head.

There were sounds coming from the cafeteria. Was someone coming? Did they know I was out there?

"Lay down," I said. "Pretend you're sleeping."

"Lucy, you're freaking me out," Austin said.

My hands tightened into fists. I would knock him out if he didn't listen.

"Please. I'll explain as soon as I can," I said lowering myself down onto the mattress.

My heart was still racing. It felt like my body was

shaking. No one would believe I was asleep. Never. No way.

I pulled the thicker blanket over my body and hoped that would hide my movements.

Whoever was out there was coming closer. I could tell by the increasing volume of their footsteps.

Each step was like a thud of the axe being swung. It was almost as though I could feel the blade hitting my body.

The footsteps stopped outside the door. Could whoever was out there hear my heart pounding against the inside of my chest like a drum?

The footsteps padded softly as they continued down the hall. My eyes widened.

Oh, God. The cup.

CHAPTER TWENTY-THREE

It was several hours later when I told the others what I'd seen. Even though I couldn't see outside, I was almost certain it would be morning soon.

Mallory's eyes were red from crying. Marty had his hand on her shoulder and looked like he was going to throw up.

"White powder, huh?" Austin said. "Are you sure?"

"I'm positive," I said.

"Did you touch it?" Austin asked looking at my fingers as if he was afraid they were going to fall right off my hand.

I shook my head. "All I know is that we have to get out of here."

"I don't think they're going to let us leave." Noah frowned. "It's going to look suspicious."

"Why would they poison him?" Mallory said her voice squeaky and hoarse.

Austin lowered his voice. "It seems like they're trying to keep the creatures satisfied. Feeding them so they stay away."

"That'll just have them keep coming back for more," Noah said.

"We're going to die here, aren't we?" Mallory asked.

Marty squeezed her closer. "We're not going to die here. We won't let that happen, right?"

"Yeah, we're not going to die," Austin said pulling out his gun. "We'll do whatever we have to do."

There was a sharp knock at the door and Austin quickly tucked his gun away just as the doorknob turned. Lucas grinned as he stared at us.

"Oh, good," Lucas said. "You're all awake."

"Yeah, we haven't been up long," Austin said as he turned his lips upward. "When one of us wakes up, we all wake up."

Lucas chuckled. "I know how that is. I hear every creak and squeak in this place. Sometimes it's quite difficult to get a good night's rest."

"I can only imagine how it must be for you," Austin said.

There was a long silence before Lucas placed his hands together and took another step into the room.

"There's something I wanted to talk to the five of you about," Lucas said in a velvety voice.

"Oh?" Austin said cocking his head to the side.

"It's about your friend, Bradley." Lucas's eyebrows drooped. "We were wondering if any of you might have known what he might have wanted in the event of his death."

Austin narrowed his eyes. "What do you mean exactly?"

"Do you think he would have wanted to be cremated?" Lucas asked.

"I don't think so," I said speaking quickly. "His family was Catholic."

Lucas bowed his head in understanding. "I'll send Samuel and a few others to acquire a casket. We'll have a service for him around noon if that suits you?"

Lucas looked at each one of us in turn. He wasn't going to move until someone answered.

"Sure," I said glancing at Mallory. Her head was lowered and tears were dripping down into her lap.

Lucas nodded and turned to leave. He stopped in the doorway and turned slightly.

"One more thing," he said. "I'm afraid it's going to have to be a closed casket. Whatever he had gone through hadn't been kind."

"What do you mean?" I asked knowing full well why the casket was going to be closed.

I could feel Austin's eyes burning a hole into the back of my head. I should have kept my mouth closed.

"It's why we didn't want you to see him," Lucas said lowering his gaze. "I really don't feel comfortable describing it. It would just be too painful and you all have already been through so much." Lucas cleared his throat and turned away again. "Breakfast should be ready in a few minutes."

Lucas had left the door open putting an end to our discussion.

"We'll leave after the service," Austin said in a voice that floated through the room like a feather.

"How?" Noah asked.

"I'm not sure yet," Austin said tapping his hip. "But one way or another we're leaving."

Mallory sniffed back her tears. "We won't survive out there."

"We can and we will," Austin said confidently.

We sat through breakfast in mostly silence. There were a few whispers back and forth between the others but meals, for the most part, had been quiet.

"I'm so sorry for your loss," Bev said placing her hand on my shoulder and then on Mallory's.

"Thanks," I said.

"Didn't know him, but he seemed like a decent man," Bev added.

I shrugged and Austin's eyes widened. I drew in a deep sniff that stung my brain.

"Sorry," I said hoping my eyes were as glassy as I was trying to make them be. "This is all just so difficult."

"I understand, dear," Bev said. "You two should take the day off. I'll manage things in the kitchen just fine without you." She lowered herself down closer to my ear. "Did it all myself before you two arrived."

Bev patted me on the back but all I could do was wonder if she'd been out there with the others hacking Bradley into pieces. I looked around the room but I couldn't remember who I'd seen. The only ones that I knew for sure had been Lucas and Samuel.

Monsters. Horrible, disgusting monsters.

They were the ones that should have been fed to the creatures. Lucas had acted like he was a religious man, but was he? Maybe the two of them, Lucas and Samuel had just holed up at the church after the creatures came and weren't actually affiliated with it at all.

Samuel smiled at me. I hadn't realized I'd been staring at him. I swallowed hard and looked away letting a slow breath escape from between my lips to calm myself.

"Excuse me," I said offering a nod to everyone around. I placed my hand on my stomach and walked quickly from the room.

My stomach was swirling. Was Samuel smiling like that as he sliced into Bradley? How could he do that to a human being and, then, sit there eating breakfast with everyone as if nothing happened?

I went up the stairs and out of the church. No one tried to stop me.

I drew in a breath as if I'd been drowning. The sun beat down on the top of my head, warming me instantly. It was higher in the sky than I'd expected. Breakfast had been late which meant it wouldn't be long before it would be time for the service.

A service led by a man that killed Bradley. A man that stood there watching his son chop him into pieces.

It was disgusting.

I couldn't be there.

I didn't want to be there.

I wasn't sure how I'd be able to hold it together. We should have been miles away from this place. It would be better to die fighting for our lives against the creatures than stuck inside with murderers.

I sat down on the steps and stared at the road. It wasn't that long ago cars would have been parked there to come to mass.

I could almost see the elderly women in their pressed pale blue skirts and their hair freshly done. The men would have nice suits and smile as they took the arms of their wives and guided them up the stairs.

Families would arrive a bit late and the mothers would look around praying their children would behave.

Never in a million years would they have guessed what would have happened inside the walls of the church. Never would they have imagined a man would get chopped to bits in the garden at the side of the church.

"Hey," Austin said cautiously stepping in front of my line of sight. "You okay?"

"I felt sick," I said.

His face dropped with panic as he reached out and touched my forehead. "The food? Did you see powder in your water?"

I shook my head. His concern for me warmed my heart and I remembered why we needed to fight. I couldn't let them take another of us.

We'd agreed we wouldn't eat much. Just enough so that they wouldn't be suspicious and since we were grieving, we hoped we'd be able to get away with it, although it wouldn't work for long.

"It's not that. I'm just sick from what I saw," I said keeping my voice low.

The visions of losing my mom and dad still haunted me, now I could add another to the list.

"I'm so sorry you had to see that," Austin said sitting down next to me. He put his arm around my shoulder and held me close.

"Aren't they going to wonder where you are?" I asked.

"I told them I was going to check on you," he said.

"We should just go," I said. "Get the others and leave."

Austin cocked his head to the side. "What about the service?"

"Argh," I groaned. "I don't know. How do we even do this? You know they aren't going to just let us leave. I just need a break away from all this to clear my head."

Austin placed a light kiss on the top of my head. "We're going to get out of this."

"How can you be so sure?"

"Because we're armed. I'm ninety percent sure they're not," Austin said.

I shook my head. "We don't even have a plan."

"We're just going to walk out. We'll go to the SUV and drive off."

"Before night? Did you move the SUV?"

"No, never got a chance. Do you want to wait until morning?" Austin asked.

I lowered my face into my hands. "I don't know. I just don't know."

"Go back inside," Austin said. "I'll go check the SUV."

"You can't," I said grabbing his arm. "They'll see you. It's too risky."

Austin pressed his fingertips to his temple. He knew I was right.

"Okay," he said. "We'll leave at dusk right before the creatures come out. They won't want to follow us. It'll be too risky for them."

I thought over his plan. We'd be driving through the night again which wasn't ideal but it probably would be our best chance to escape.

I sucked in a deep breath and released it slowly. "Okay. Let's tell the others."

CHAPTER TWENTY-FOUR

Lucas led us out toward the cemetery in the backyard of the church. The headstones were crumbling and some of them looked like there were about to sink into the ground. Maybe the creature's tunnels below were pulling them downward.

It was an old cemetery. Based on the years on the headstones, it hadn't been used in years.

There was a casket on the ground next to a hole that wasn't even close to six feet deep. Someone had decorated both the ground and the casket with flowers, many of which were wilted.

A headstone made of wood had been stuck into the ground at the top of the hole. They hadn't even bothered to ask how to spell Bradley's name and had gotten it wrong, not that I was going to say anything.

"We're all gathered here to celebrate the life of

Bradley," Lucas said holding his hands up at his sides. "Please, gather around."

Everyone was there. None of them looked as though they wanted to be except for Lucas.

I scanned the area as he began reading from the bible. It felt like Lucas didn't know the first thing about conducting a funeral and listening to his voice was only making my insides boil.

"Does anyone have anything they'd like to say about our beloved, Bradley?" Lucas asked shifting his gaze toward me.

I moved my head slightly side to side. If I even tried, I'd break down into tears for so many reasons.

Mallory stepped forward and a lump lodged itself in the back of my throat.

"I do," she said pressing her palms against her thighs.

"Go on," Lucas said taking a step back.

"Um," Mallory said keeping her eyes down. "I loved Bradley. He was an asshole, but he didn't deserve this. This is not how it should have ended. He donated money to Humane Society and for the most part, he was kind to me. Much kinder than others have been. He wasn't verbally abusive like my last boyfriend."

Mallory's shoulders dropped and she wiped away her tears. She pressed her fingertips to her lips for a moment before clearing her throat.

"Anyway," she said reaching out to touch the casket even though she knew he wasn't inside. "I love you, Bradley. Rest in peace."

He wasn't going to rest in peace in this graveyard. In fact, I hoped he would find his way to haunt both Lucas and Samuel for the rest of their lives.

"Very touching," Lucas said. "Anyone else?"

Lucas concluded the ceremony by making the sigh of the cross. He folded his hands in front of his chest as he pasted a gentle smile on his face.

"Bev has prepared a lovely lunch," Lucas said gesturing at the church. "If you wouldn't mind, please follow her back to the cafeteria."

My feet didn't move. I stared at the casket. Lucas's unblinking eyes were on me.

"Is there something else?" he asked.

I swallowed hard. "Aren't you going to lower him into the ground?"

"We will," Lucas said. "Later."

"Why later?" I asked.

I just couldn't keep my mouth closed even though Austin was pulling on my arm. Lucas gestured at the others to keep going. Apparently, everyone had stopped and waited for his response.

Lucas stepped up next to me and looked down into my eyes. I saw nothing but ice cold emptiness.

"It's difficult to watch a loved one being lowered

into the ground," Lucas explained. "Especially, when we don't have the tools to do it smoothly."

"Oh," I said biting my cheek so I didn't say anything more.

"I know this is a difficult time for all of you," Lucas said placing his hand on my shoulder. I flinched ever so slightly but I was sure it was enough that he'd noticed. He let his hand fall away. "It's a different world now, though, isn't it?"

I nodded. It was different because of the creatures but I wasn't sure if that was what he was referring to.

"Everyone has to do what they must to survive." Lucas flicked his eyes in my direction. "We all must make sacrifices to help one another, don't you think?"

A tight-lipped smile was the most I could muster for his words that made my stomach swirl like a washing machine. Sacrifices. Lucas made me sick.

I was counting the minutes until dusk.

After our quiet meal, Bev poured us each a cup of coffee and passed out a single brownie to each of us.

Samuel quietly announced they'd be going on a supply run. He walked over and asked Noah and Marty if they were up for joining him.

Neither Austin nor I had gotten a chance to tell them our plan. My heart sank when they both accepted.

Perhaps it didn't really matter because they'd be

back before dusk. Samuel patted them both on the back before walking around the table and stopping behind Austin.

"Austin," Samuel said. He sounded like a snake the way the name slithered out between his lips. "I was wondering if you'd be up for joining us on a run today."

"Not today," Austin said barely turning to look at him.

"Hmm," Samuel said. "We could really use your help out there."

The muscles in Austin's face tightened. "I'm sorry. It's not a good day."

"You sure? Might help take your mind off of things." It didn't seem like Samuel was going to take no for an answer and I knew Austin wasn't going to back down.

My body tensed worrying that this might be the moment we'd need to make our move.

"I'm positive. Tomorrow," Austin said.

Samuel opened his mouth but snapped it shut when Austin turned and met his eyes. He wanted him to see that he wasn't going to be changing his mind.

I bit back my smile when Samuel held up his hand and took a step back. He'd gotten the message.

"Okay," Samuel said pushing back his shoulders. "Tomorrow."

"Yeah, tomorrow," Austin said unable to hide the tinge of sourness to his tone.

Noah shot him a strange look. He knew something was up but he was smart enough not to draw any kind of attention to that fact.

After everyone cleared out of the cafeteria, Austin told Mallory the plan. She threw her arms around his neck and hugged him as if he'd just told her she'd won the lottery.

"Thank you, Austin," she said taking a quick step back. Mallory lowered her voice. "Sorry. I'm just so happy to hear that. I hate it here."

"Don't thank me just yet," Austin said.

Mallory frowned and shook her head. "If anyone can get us out of here, it's you."

"I appreciate your vote of confidence," Austin said his face blank.

Mallory smiled. But her fears had resurfaced. She could tell just as well as I could that Austin was nervous about what was going to happen. He seemed afraid... worried... that something was going to go wrong.

"You sshould go get some rest," Austin advised.

"Right," Mallory said. "What about you two? Shouldn't you rest, too? We don't get enough sleep out there."

"We should," Austin said. "But I'd like to talk to Lucy first."

Mallory raised a brow. "Oh," she said flashing me a wink, "I get it."

"Oh, no," Austin said.

"Yeah, it's not like that," I said even though I had no idea what it was like. It just felt awkward with her thinking what she was thinking.

Mallory leaned closer. "There's a coat closet right next to the restroom."

She bounced on the balls of her feet as she turned away from us. After six steps her shoulders dropped and her pace slowed. It was like she remembered the horrible reality we were trapped inside.

"What did you want to talk to me about?" I asked turning to Austin.

Austin's head lowered but his eyes shifted to meet mine. "Mallory was right. I just wanted some time to be with you."

"What?" I asked looking around as if someone was watching us.

"Well, it's just that shit might hit the fan and I don't want to have any regrets," Austin said. "I'm stressed and worried and I just want to be alone with you. Is that so wrong?"

Austin took a step closer and my heart skipped a beat. There were too many emotions running through my body that the only thing I could feel was just how overwhelmed I was with everything.

What if something went wrong? What if this was the last chance I would get to be alone with Austin?

I grabbed his hand and smiled. There wasn't anything that could stop me from leading him to the coat closet.

Maybe it was wrong. Maybe the timing was terrible, but being alone with Austin helped me forget the world around us and that made me feel like I could take on anything. It helped to remind me what I was fighting for.

I opened the closet door and peeked inside. There wasn't anything in the room except a few empty hangers that had been pushed to the side.

I stepped inside the room, smiling as I pulled him with me.

CHAPTER TWENTY-FIVE

We didn't speak.

His arms were around my waist seconds after the door softly clicked closed. I drew in a sharp breath as he roughly pulled me against his body.

"It's not fair," he said in a husky voice.

"What's not fair?" I asked trying to see his face but the room was pitch black. I probably wasn't even looking into his eyes.

"How things are," Austin said kissing the side of my neck sending hot tingles over the top of my skull and down my spine.

His touch made my body feel lighter. Just being close to Austin was enough to make me feel intoxicated.

"They feel pretty good to me," I said as his hand

moved up the side of my body and over my breast. I bit my lip. "Really good."

"But it should be different. We shouldn't have to sneak off to be together," Austin said his voice losing a bit of passion as it filled with seriousness. "It shouldn't be days or weeks before I can do something like this."

Austin lifted my body slightly and pressed me against the back wall. It was just the right amount of roughness

He grabbed my wrists and held them with one hand over my head. The fingers of his free hand slid down my body until he got to the hem of my shirt.

Austin gripped it so tightly I could feel the fabric wrinkling against my body. He wanted it off but he wasn't going to undress me in the coat closet when anyone could just walk in.

His hand glided up until he found the thin fabric of my bra and slid his hand inside. I felt so hot I was afraid I was going to stick to the wall.

"Oh, Austin," I said letting my head fall back into the wall. It felt like I was absolutely under his spell.

"I need you," Austin whispered into my ear.

"I need you, too," I said letting all the emotions inside of me fuel my desire.

I tried to move my hands down to undo the button on my pants but he felt my pull and held me tighter.

His fingers moved down and he popped the button. My heart skipped a beat as the sound of my zipper being undone filled the air.

I couldn't stand it. I wanted to move my arms. Touch him. Feel him. But it wasn't long before I felt him in a very satisfying way.

Austin held me up against the wall as he rocked into me. Pin-pricks of pleasure zapped up and down my body from head to toe sending me to a plane of pleasure I hadn't ever experienced.

It was strange but exciting not to be able to move. He was controlling every movement and it felt amazing to just let go. I didn't have to think about anything. All I had to do was feel.

Our bodies thudded softly against the wall. My breaths slipped between my parted lips as I ached for more.

"I love you, Lucy," Austin said. The sound of my name on his lips scorched my already searing veins.

I couldn't stand it. I couldn't take another movement.

The pleasure rippled down my neck, over my chest and came together where our bodies met. I exhaled as my shoulders rolled forward.

A soft moan started to squeeze its way out of my mouth but I bit down so hard on my lip I was afraid I might draw blood. I wanted to call out his name but I couldn't. I couldn't.

Austin growled as he pressed me harder to the wall for a moment. It was like his body had frozen solid as he enjoyed his own moment of release.

A soft chuckled bounced against my ear. I couldn't help but smile into the darkness.

"What's so funny?" I asked.

"I've never done anything like that in my entire life," Austin said. "It's like I'm a different person, but still I'm the same."

"I know what you mean," I said as I pulled my pants back on and smoothed my hands over my shirt.

I felt Austin's fingertips brush feather-soft against my cheek. "Are you okay?"

"Yeah, of course," I said. "Why wouldn't I be?"

"I don't want to be too rough. Something took over me," Austin said.

"No," I said lighting placing my hand on top of his. "It was perfect."

The truth was it was more than okay. I could take it. But now that it was over, everything outside the door was flooding back and resting itself on top of my shoulders.

I could handle whatever Austin could dish out. What I couldn't handle was the world outside. The creatures. The murderers we were staying with.

I couldn't wait until we were back in the SUV miles away from this place.

We'd figure out what to do. We knew the sound the creatures didn't like and we already knew they didn't like the light. Surely we'd be able to build something where we could be safe.

First, we just had to get away from the church.

Austin wrapped his arms around me again squeezing me tightly. "You know I really do love you, right?"

"I do know," I said resting my cheek against his chest. "And I love you, too."

"If for some reason something should go wrong—"

"Don't," I said placing my fingertips over his mouth. "Don't even say it. I don't want to hear it. It's going to be fine. It has to be."

Austin's hand wrapped around my wrist and he slowly moved my fingers away from his mouth. I thought he was going to finish his sentence but he didn't.

"You're right. I won't let anything happen to you," Austin said.

"And I won't let anything happen to you," I said standing on my tiptoes to kiss his cheek. "Or Marty, Noah, or Mallory."

"If you have to pull the trigger," Austin said and I

wished I could see his expression. "You'll be able to do it, right?"

The thumping in my chest increased. Could I? I would have to. "I think so."

"It's not a think so kind of response. You may have to act fast," Austin said. I could hear the seriousness in his tone. "Tell me you'll be able to do it."

"I will," I said releasing a shaky breath. He didn't seem convinced.

"Just remember what they did to Bradley. They aren't good people," Bradley said.

I chewed my cheek. "Do you think it's going to come down to that? Guns? Bullets?"

"I hope to hell not," Austin said. "But we need to be prepared for the worst. That's how we made it this far."

"You consider us having been prepared?" I asked.

"As prepared as we could be, yes," Austin said.

Maybe he was right. The lights had been what had kept us alive. "If so, it's only because of you."

"We should get back out there," Austin said. "Before everyone wonders where we've gone off to."

"Do you think they're back?" I asked.

Austin took my hand into his. "I don't know. Let's go find out. I'm anxious to get the hell out of this place."

"Me too," I said.

The light stung my eyes as Austin opened the coat closet door. Something hit the tip of my shoe and ping-ponged on the floor.

I blinked several times before realizing what it was. It was Bradley's cup.

CHAPTER TWENTY-SIX

I gasped and covered my mouth with my hands. My fingers were shaking uncontrollably.

"Oh, my God." The words were soft and they bounced together harshly. "They know. They know that I know what they did."

"Shit," Austin said looking like he wanted to put his fist through the wall. "Not only that, but somehow they knew we were in the closet. There might not be anything they don't know."

"What are we going to do?" I asked pushing back the tears.

Austin ran his hand down his face pulling on his chin. "We're going to get Mallory and wait outside for Noah and Marty."

He placed his hand on my back and guided me

back toward our room. Austin hastily turned the knob and pushed open the door.

"Shit!" Austin said slamming his palm against the wall. "Let's go."

We walked down the hall opening every door, not caring if anyone was inside. Every room, however, was empty.

"I don't like this," I said. It wasn't just because of the cup that I knew something was wrong, I could feel it in the air.

We moved quickly through the entire basement. Bev was in the kitchen working on dinner.

"Have you seen Mallory?" Austin asked.

Bev's hands shook as she picked up a plate and moved her head side to side. The woman knew exactly where she was but she wasn't going to tell us. It seemed as though she wanted to but fear was keeping her lips sealed.

We charged up the stairs. It wasn't until we got to the top that I heard the organ playing.

Austin stepped in front of me protectively even though there wasn't anyone around. My eyes moved around as though I expected all of them to jump out at us with axes in hand.

Our feet took us toward the music. It felt like there was a tarantula crawling across my back.

The music was haunting. Bone-chilling.

Austin pulled out his gun but kept it behind as his back as we stepped into the church. Lucas was standing in front of the altar and there were several people sitting in the pews staring at him.

"Join us," Lucas said and they turned around to watch us approach. Lucas stepped to the side.

"No!" I gasped.

"Mallory's already here," Lucas said. "And the others will be back shortly."

Mallory was gagged and tied to the altar with thin pieces of rope wrapped around her wrists and ankles. Her head was turned to the side, redness and terror filled her eyes.

Austin let out a breath as his jaw tensed. "Let her go."

"I can't do that," Lucas said.

Mallory looked like she was trying to say something but I couldn't even attempt to make out her words with the sounds of the organ pounding through the room.

"Please, won't you join us?" Lucas said gesturing toward the pews. He took the radio from his belt. "They're here. Come on back."

The church was darker than it had been the last time I'd been inside. I wasn't sure how close it was to night, but maybe it was just a cloudy day.

"I think we're good here," Austin said.

Mallory tried to kick her legs but they barely moved. The small little thuds the heels of her feet made against the wooden alter were barely noticeable.

"Why don't you let her go," Austin said. "Nobody wants any of this. We'll just part ways peacefully."

"Peacefully, huh?" Lucas asked with a snort. "Why would you want to leave? There's nothing out there."

"We just think it's time to get back on the road," Austin said.

Lucas started pacing in front of Mallory. My heart sank as the tears streamed down her face. It seemed like she was worried. Worried that we'd leave.

"Something has you worried," Lucas said clasping his hands in front of his chest. "We're good people. We only do good things."

Lucas was delusional. Maybe he didn't know what I saw outside and only knew I'd moved the cup.

It wasn't like I knew what had been in the cup or that I could even prove there'd been anything in it at all. I'd bet my life it had been something that killed Bradley but when it came down to it, it was my word versus his. His followers would believe him or maybe they already knew what he'd done. Maybe they didn't care.

"I'd just like to talk to you all... explain," Lucas said as he started to pace again. He stepped out of the way so that I could see Mallory's terrified face again. Good people. Ha. "They'll be here any moment."

It was less than ten seconds when the doors of the church squeaked open and quickly closed. I turned back and saw Samuel and the others that had been with them walking behind Marty and Noah. The only one that wasn't in the church was Bev.

"Ah ha! And there they are," Lucas said waving his hand. "Come on, come on, join us."

Marty and Noah stepped up behind Austin and me. Samuel and the other stayed behind them blocking our exit.

"What's going on?" Noah asked Austin.

"I don't know," Austin said keeping his voice low. "But we're going to get the hell out of here."

"We can't leave her," Marty said.

Austin nodded.

"Come closer," Lucas said. "Don't be shy."

I didn't think any of us wanted to take another step in Lucas's direction but somehow we were going to have to get to Mallory. We'd have to find a way to free her before we could leave.

"Look," Austin said. "Just let us go and we can all get back to our lives. Nobody wants any trouble here."

"Are you trouble?" Lucas asked cocking his head to the side. "Are you going to cause us some kind of trouble?"

Austin shook his head. "That's not at all what I meant. It's just you said you were good people, right? Well, then, let us go. Let Mallory go."

"I can't do that. I wish I could but she's been caught breaking the rules," Lucas said.

"Rules?" I asked. "What rules?"

"We caught her and Marty in the coat closet," Lucas said. "This is a church. A place of God."

"You said you were going to let it go!" Marty squawked.

Austin took a step closer to the altar. "God wouldn't approve of you tying her up on the altar, would he?"

Lucas looked like he'd been punched in the stomach. His mouth dropped open but he quickly snapped it shut and drew in a deep inhale as he composed himself.

"People have been executed for far less," Lucas said.

"You're going to execute her?" Austin asked keeping a calmness to his voice that I knew I wouldn't be able to manage. "For being in the coat closet?"

Lucas frowned as he looked toward his feet. He hesitated before raising his head up again.

"Yes," he said clearly. "And when we finish with Mallory, it'll be her next."

Someone grabbed my hands and pulled them hard

behind my back. I tried to jerk my arms free but the grip on me only tightened.

"Let me go!" I yelled.

"She not only broke the rules, sharing her bed and what not but she also is a snoop," Lucas said. "Sneaking around places she shouldn't be."

"I didn't do anything!" I shouted as I whipped my shoulders back and forth. "Let. Me. Go."

Lucas held his hand up and the room became silent except for my grunts. "Bring her up here."

"No," Austin said stepping in front of me. "That's not going to happen."

Lucas held up a blade and placed it at Mallory's neck. "Oh, its happening or she dies."

"You said you were going to execute her anyway," Austin said and Mallory's eyes widened.

Lucas started to drag the blade along Mallory's neck. A small trickle of dark red blood oozed down the side of her neck.

"First, they were to be judged," Lucas said. "But I see we may not have time for that."

"Okay, okay!" Austin said but he didn't move.

We were running out of time. Something had to happen or it was going to be over, likely for all of us.

"Come," Lucas said straightening his spine and pulling the blade away from Mallory's neck. "Come forth to be judged."

"Okay, I will," I said but I kept my feet planted firmly as I pushed back against whoever was holding me. "But let me come on my own. I don't need to be pushed around like this."

Lucas stared for a moment and flicked a finger at the person behind me. Blood started to circulate through my body against as they let go. My arms and hands tingled but quickly life came back to them.

"What are you doing?" Austin said as I stepped around him.

"I don't know," I said but I knew. I knew exactly what I was going to do but what it would mean for us... well, that I didn't know.

I drew in a breath as I walked up the small set of stairs before the altar. Lucas smirked as I stared into his eyes.

I stepped up beside him and lowered my head. "Forgive me for my sins."

"We shall see," Lucas said.

What Lucas didn't know was that I wasn't talking to him. I was talking to my God.

I reached behind my back and pulled out my gun. Someone screamed in the pew to my right as I aimed the barrel between Lucas's eyes.

I didn't hesitate.

I pulled the trigger.

CHAPTER TWENTY-SEVEN

Blood splattered and rained down on me. Lucas's empty eyes were glued to me as he dropped to the ground.

"Dad!" Samuel shouted as I knelt down and picked up the blade Lucas had dropped.

Half of the people were running out of the church. Some crying and wailing as they fled.

Austin turned and pointed his gun at Samuel as Marty and Noah aimed theirs around the room at the others who stuck around. My hand shook as I turned to cut Mallory free.

I cut the rope at her hands and she rubbed at her wrists. Her eyes were popping out of her head and it looked like she was trying to say something. I removed her gag but I couldn't understand the word she'd worked to croak out.

"What?" I asked as I moved to her feet.

"Dark!" she said pointing to the windows.

No one had turned the lights on and the church was about to be swallowed by the impending darkness.

"Dammit!" I said helping her down from the altar.

"What are you going to do?" Samuel shouted. "Kill us all?"

"We just want to leave," Austin said.

Samuel smirked even though his eyes were filled with sadness. "It's time for you to be judged."

Austin adjusted his aim and shook his head as he narrowed his eyes. "Just let us go."

"It's not like there's anything you can do," Noah said.

"Oh, yeah?" an older man said balling his hands into fists. He started charging toward Noah. "I'll show you what I'm going to do."

He was less than a foot away when Austin hit him in the chest. The man dropped to his knees and all the confidence he had only seconds ago poured out of him.

"What did you do that for?" the man asked as he raised his bloody hands up. "You shot me." He looked over at Samuel. "I'm going to die, aren't I?"

"Probably," Samuel said without emotion.

"Are you going to feed me to them?" the man asked.

Samuel glanced briefly at Austin. A deep, evil smirk grew on Samuel's face. "Probably."

"No," the man begged shaking his head as he turned to Noah. "Don't let him do that to me. I don't want to be their food."

"Why were you doing it? Why did you do it to Bradley?" I asked.

The man turned to me. "What choice did I have? What choice did any of us have? I did what I had to do to survive."

He pressed his hands to his wound and stared at the blood again. His skin turned as white as a ghost.

"This is your fault," he said jabbing his bloody finger in Samuel's direction. "I hope you join your father in hell!"

Something slammed into the wall behind us. A crack sprouted in the stained glass window and spread out like growing vines.

Mallory gripped my arm and squeaked. "Maybe I should have taken a gun."

"Bradley's gun," I whispered.

"What?" Mallory asked looking at me sideways.

"They must have taken it," I said.

It was as though Samuel had read my mind when he grabbed Austin and pressed Bradley's gun to this side of his head.

"Put your guns down," Samuel ordered as another

creature slammed into the wall. "Or I swear to God I'll shoot him."

Bit of wood and dust rained down from the shaking roof. The creatures were up there, crawling around and pounding their claws into the wood.

"Someone turn on the damn lights!" Samuel shouted.

A creature burst in through the wall and tumbled on the ground toward Marty. He put three bullets in it... one in the chest, the shoulder and the last in the head before it stopped moving.

"Give me your guns!" Samuel shouted with urgency and desperation saturating his tone.

"No," Noah said turning and shooting Samuel in the head.

He started to fall and pulled the trigger, but the bullet missed Austin and went through the wall several inches away.

"That was risky," Austin said taking the gun from Samuel's hand.

"Yeah," Noah said with a soft chuckle that was rattled by his nerves.

Austin stood next to me and put his hand on my back. They still hadn't turned the lights on and something told me they weren't going to.

"We gotta get out of here," Austin said looking from side to side at the shaking walls.

"How are we going to do that?" Mallory whimpered. "We can't go out there."

Marty stepped up next to her and put his arm around her. They looked at one another before embracing.

"When did this happen?" I asked.

"Does it matter?" Marty said taking Mallory's hand. "Let's get the fuck out of here."

"Marty! Watch your language," I scolded and we both smiled despite the worry we were both feeling. I looked over my shoulder and pulled on Austin. "He's right though, we really do need to get out of here."

Austin nodded. "Remember, those things can't see."

"Their hearing is sensitive," Mallory said. "They don't like high-pitched noises."

"We need to be absolutely silent," Austin said.

"Or screaming our lungs out," Mallory added.

I wasn't sure if it was going to help considering the creatures were still all over the walls trying to make their way inside. Somehow, they knew we were inside.

We moved through the church quickly and as quietly as we could. They were still pounding and slamming against the walls but we didn't hear anything at the front door.

Opening the door would make a sound. They'd rush us before we could even make it to the SUV.

"We need to turn the lights on," I whispered mostly mouthing the words. It was the only way I could think of to get them to leave.

"Where is the SUV?" Noah asked.

"I never moved it," Austin said. "As long as they didn't tamper with it, it's where we left it."

"We still have to get to it," I said scratching away the prickles at the back of my neck.

There was a noise behind us that was so loud it sounded like the building was being sucked into the ground. Noah turned and pointed his gun in the darkness.

"They're coming," Noah whispered.

I could see their shadows stretching out as they moved around and tore through the aisles. They were looking for us. If Noah had to shoot, it would draw their attention, all of them, to our location.

Mallory covered her mouth with both hands. There wasn't anything we could do but stand there... silent... still and hope to God they stayed in the other room.

I could see the glow coming from the basement. Whoever was down there was attempting to protect themselves as best as they could.

The sounds of the creatures grew louder as they tore their way through the church. With each crashing thud, my body jerked. My heart pounded so loud I was sure they could hear it.

We had to do something. I pointed at the light in the basement, but Austin shook his head.

He was worried about what would happen to us if we went down. It wasn't like they were going to welcome us with open arms after we'd killed Lucas and Samuel. Then again, after what the man had said, maybe they would have.

The volume from the boombox increased. The screeches became more frequent and the thuds lessened. Were they leaving?

One of the creatures howled. I could hear them scampering out of the destroyed church.

Then, there was nothing. Just us standing there frozen like marble statues.

"Let's go," Austin said opening the door. The hinges creaked as he peered out.

There was movement in the basement but it didn't sound like they were coming for us. Not that we could take a risk.

We stepped out into the darkness, holding onto one another. It was like we were afraid if we let go, we'd float up into the atmosphere never to be seen again.

I turned around and looked at the mostly destroyed church. There were parts that were still standing but much of it was not. The lights probably wouldn't work and if they did, it likely wouldn't be sufficient.

We needed to make it to the SUV.

Our footsteps sounded loud as they pounded across the pavement. There was more movement in the shadows not far from where we were. The sounds from the church wouldn't be loud enough to help keep them away.

Somewhere in the distance one of the creatures called out a howl unlike any I've heard before. The rustling in the shadows dissipated. I could hear the creatures running this way and that, disappearing from the area.

We stood absolutely still as they ran toward the cries in the distance. It was like they were being called.

"They're leaving?" Mallory asked as something dashed past us in the darkness.

Austin held up his gun but he didn't need to use it because the creatures kept running. It seemed like they didn't care about us any longer.

"What's going on?" Noah asked.

"Not sure," Austin said. "But let's keep moving. They might change their mind and decide they're still hungry."

It had felt like we'd traveled miles. A wave of relief washed over me when I saw the SUV still in its spot.

We all climbed inside and the familiar smell made me tear up. Hints of my mother were still there.

"Where do we go now?" Mallory asked cozying up next to Marty.

It was going to take a while to adjust to seeing my brother with his arm around Mallory. When he caught me looking at him, he just shot me a smile. He was happy to be back in our mom's SUV too.

"Anywhere we want," Austin said.

"Far away from here," I said.

Austin shifted the SUV into drive and pulled away from the curb and sped out of town.

CHAPTER TWENTY-EIGHT

My eyelids fluttered open. The sun had been up for at least an hour but Austin hadn't woke me.

I looked over my shoulder into the backseat. Noah was stretched out on the middle seat with his cap over his face. Marty was slouched to the side with Mallory sleeping on his chest.

"Good morning," Austin said softly.

"Is it?" I asked.

He reached over and took my hand into his. Austin smiled at me and I couldn't help but grin back. It felt good to be away from the church.

"You must be tired," I said nodding at the steering wheel. "Want me to take over for a bit?"

"Nah," Austin said. "I don't even know where I'm going."

I noticed the gas gauge was low. "We're going to need gas soon."

"Right now, I'm just enjoying the country scenery," Austin said. There was a partial silo standing and I wondered if he was thinking about his extinct home.

"We'll figure it out later," I said spotting one of the creatures holes in one of the fields. "Do you think they're gone?"

Austin shook his head. "Don't get your hopes up."

"It was weird though, right?" I asked.

"Yeah, it was."

We drove a few more miles in near silence. The heavy breaths and light snores from the others were almost enough to put me back to sleep. It was amazing that Austin was able to keep his eyes open and the SUV on the road.

"What's that?" I asked pointing at a black dot in the sky. It looked like it was moving toward us.

"Hmm," Austin said squinting at the dot. "Is it a helicopter?"

As it grew, I could both see and hear that he was right. "Is it coming for us?"

"I'm not sure," Austin said glancing in the rearview mirror as if he were afraid we were being followed. A trap. But there wasn't anything behind us. "Wake them up."

I nodded as I reached back and hit Noah on the knee. "Wake up, Noah."

"Go away," he groaned.

"Hey," Austin said. "There's a helicopter."

"Huh?" Noah said. He sat up and pulled his hat over his wild, messy hair. "What is it doing?"

Austin shook his head.

The helicopter had moved fast and was almost above us. Noah reached back and woke Marty and Mallory.

"What do we do?" Mallory asked. "It's just hovering there."

"It's military," Noah said.

"That doesn't mean anything," Austin said. "Haven't you learned anything?"

Noah shrugged. "I know, I'm just saying."

The helicopter started to descend into a field to our left.

"What should we do?" I asked gripping Austin's hand tighter.

Austin swallowed hard and slowed the SUV. He shifted into park and turned to face all of us.

"I can floor it and try to get us out of here or we can see what they want. Let's take a vote," Austin said.

Noah stared out of the window. "There's a pilot, co-pilot and two men getting out. They're armed and they're coming this way."

"We're armed too," I said flicking my eyes toward the men. They didn't look like they were up to anything. Their guns were on their shoulders but they did seem hesitant. "It looks like they are afraid of us."

"Stay here," Austin said checking his gun before he placed his hand on the door handle.

I grabbed his arm and pulled him back to me. I pressed my lips to his and then, let go.

The second he closed his door, I placed my hand on my door handle. "Wait here."

Marty groaned and hit the car seat as I exited the SUV.

Austin glanced back over his shoulder and shook his head. "I told you to stay in the car."

"I know, but you might need me," I said.

The men stopped about ten feet away from us. They didn't take their eyes off of us.

"Are you armed," the man on the left shouted.

"We are," Austin said.

"How many survivors?" the man asked.

"Five counting us," Austin said.

The men exchanged a surprised look. "We're U.S. Military and we're here to offer help. We have a base ten miles north. There's food, water, shelter, and the place is fortified."

"We can take you," the man on the right said gesturing toward the helicopter.

Austin shook his head. "We don't want to leave our SUV."

"I can see why," the man on the left said. "Quite the setup."

"We've had some difficult times," Austin said flatly. "We're not interested."

"We can help," the man said.

Austin chuckled but it probably hadn't been loud enough for the men to hear. "We've heard that before."

"The choice is yours," the man said as he pointed at the road. "Follow this road, make a right on highway KK and the military base is on your left. You can't miss it."

"This isn't a trick," the second man said. "If you want to survive, your odds will be best with us."

The first man nodded along with each word. "I don't know what kind of hell you've endured but you'll be safe. There are nearly two hundred survivors at the base. We will win this war and rebuild."

"We'll think about it," Austin said and the first man raised his hand.

"If you go, and I hope you do, tell the men at the gate you spoke with Sergeant Sparks," he said pointing at the name patch on his chest. He waved and took a step back. "We hope to see you again soon."

Austin nodded. We stood there watching them as they walked back to the helicopter.

"What should we do?" I asked taking his hand into mine.

Austin let out a loud sigh that dropped his shoulders. "We haven't had much luck going places have we?"

"Maybe it'll be okay. If they wanted to, they probably could have forced us to go with them," I said as my hair started to whip around my face from the wind created by the helicopter blades. "They didn't."

"Let's see what the others think," Austin said as he led me back toward the car.

After Austin told them everything, the SUV was silent as they contemplated our choice. No one had the slightest idea of what was the right thing to do.

"We can take the risk," Austin said.

"You want to go?" Noah asked.

Austin shook his head before he finished speaking. "I don't know what we should do. But we don't have a lot of options. We can't drive around forever, can we?"

"They said there are two hundred survivors," I said glancing back at Marty. I wanted to keep him safe but I wasn't sure I could do that on my own in the SUV that would eventually run out of gas. "I think we should check it out."

"Let's vote," Austin said. "Raise your hand if you want to go."

I raised my hand. Mallory locked eyes with me and raised her hand with a smile.

Austin flicked his head toward Noah but looked away as he raised his hand.

"It's three to two then," Noah said. "Guess we're going."

"Nah," Marty said raising his hand. "Four to one."

"Why don't you want to go?" I asked biting my cheek as I stared into Noah's eyes.

A short breath escaped from between his lips. "I can't do that again. I don't want to fight with people. I never want to use my gun again."

"Me either," I said. "But if we stay out here, I think odds are good we will have to."

"I'm just tired," Noah said. He flapped his hand at the road. "Let's go then."

"Noah," Austin said. "I don't want to make you do something you don't want to do."

"I'm just scared," Noah admitted.

"We all are," Austin said. "But I think they were the real deal. They didn't force us to go with them. They could have. I know it's scary as hell but we're together. We've made it this far, we're not going to give up now."

I smiled. "We need the vote to be unanimous or I don't want to go."

"Oh, God," Noah groaned. "I just didn't want to

vote yes so I could say I told you so when everything goes to shit."

I chuckled. "You can still say that."

"Fine," Noah said. "Let's check it out."

"Are you sure?" Austin asked.

Noah drew in a long breath and released it. "Yes, I'm sure."

CHAPTER TWENTY-NINE

We pulled up to the gate and the men at the gate carefully approached the SUV. Austin rolled down his window an inch or so and placed his hands loosely on the steering wheel.

"Sergeant Sparks told us to come here," Austin said as they came to the window.

The men relaxed. One of them went back and started to slide open the gate.

"You can park your car inside, there's a lot just to the left," the man with the name Renard on his name badge said.

"I'd feel more comfortable leaving it out here," Austin said. The men looked confused. "In case we want to leave."

"Um, suit yourself," Renard said with a shrug. He gestured to a spot on the dead grass several feet away from the gate. "We need to keep this road clear. Park over there."

Austin parked and looked like he was having second thoughts as he got out of the SUV. If he was, he kept his mouth closed. He grabbed my hand tightly as we walked back to the gate.

Renard held up his hand. "I have to ask... are you armed?"

"We are," Austin said. "And I told that to Sergeant Sparks."

"I need to make sure our people are safe here. There are children, families, and to be honest with you, the guns we carry kind of freak them out even though we keep them at the gate," Renard said with a slight grin. "Any chance you'd hand them over or leave them in your car?"

Noah shifted his weight from one foot to the other. He looked right into Renard's eyes. "If it weren't for our guns, sir, we wouldn't be alive right now. We need to keep ourselves safe."

Renard studied us for a long moment.

"Keep them hidden for now," Renard said in a low voice. "I saw my own amount of shit when I was trying to make my way here. But know that if you do anything to put these kind, innocent folks in harm's way, I'll blow your fucking head off, understood?"

Noah nodded and almost seemed pleased with the

way the man had responded. Like it was some kind of proof that they were who they said they were.

Renard led us passed the first several buildings. They looked like they were mostly offices of some kind. There were small sheds lined along the left side near the fence and in the middle of the large area were copious amounts of little houses. Children were playing with a red ball while parents watched them from their lawn chairs. People looked out their doors and windows as we passed through. Most of them gave us a friendly wave or smile even if they seemed apprehensive about our presence.

"How long have you been here?" Austin asked.

"Nearly since it all started. Some of the men in uniform were here since day one welcoming in the others. Many of the folks here like to keep busy so they work on building more of the houses," Renard said with a smile that quickly turned to a frown. "They're hopeful more survivors will come but it's slowed down tremendously over the last couple weeks."

"Are there other places like this out there?" Noah asked.

Renard shook his head. "Maybe but we have not heard from anyone. We're going to do what we can to get rid of those things and rebuild." Renard pushed back his shoulders. "We've eliminated hundreds, maybe even thousands and we're not going to stop."

"They're all over the world," Marty said.

"We're not going to stop," Renard repeated. "Anyway, you'll be safe here. Everyone is kind and helpful although quiet. It's still hard for everyone to process that everything is gone."

"Tell me about it," Marty muttered.

Renard lowered his head but his eyes raised up toward the horizon. "We're going to get through this. Riley will give you the rundown on this place when you're ready. She'll assign you an empty building." Renard placed his thick hand on Austin's shoulder. "You guys made it this far and that's damn impressive. We need people like you."

He scratched at his forehead and smiled as he flicked his finger at someone off to the side. A thin woman wave and walked toward us.

"This is Riley," Renard said.

"Hi," she said softly. Renard wrapped his arm around the woman's shoulder and she kissed him on the cheek. "Back to the gate?"

"Back to the gate," he said as he saluted her.

She watched him as he walked away. "My husband," she said proudly. "Let me show you around."

Riley took us around the camp and told us about each and every building. She showed us the lighting system around the fence and told us how they've been surviving.

It was sad.

It was impressive.

And somehow, I felt like we weren't alone in the world.

Riley told us about the sounds they'd heard the creatures making last night. The same ones we'd heard before they all went running.

She told us that several people in the camp believed they went back into hibernation. She also said that no one planned to let the guard down.

Riley gave us a key to our homes. Noah was fine staying alone even though Austin tried to convince him to stay with us.

"I'll be okay," Noah said. "You guys deserve some alone time and I really, really, don't want to be a third wheel."

"We could all stay together," I suggested and Marty and Mallory exchanged a glance. I couldn't help but grimace.

"That's not going to happen," Marty said.

I exhaled. "If anyone changes their mind for any reason, our door will always be open."

It wasn't that I wasn't excited to be alone with Austin because I was, it was just that I wasn't exactly comfortable with the idea of being apart from Marty. After all, it was my job to take care of him.

Austin and I closed the door to our little house. The silence felt awkward but it was somehow different. Peaceful.

We laid down in our firm full-sized mattress and listened to the world around us. I rested my head on his chest and I was pretty sure it was the first time my aching muscles relaxed in weeks. I sighed and Austin kissed the top of my head.

"We're going to be okay now," Austin said.

"How do you know?"

He squeezed his arm around me tighter. "I can feel it. Can't you? It's different."

"Yeah, I think I can," I said with a long exhale. It did feel different.

The hours seemed to fly by. Before nightfall all five of us sat outside on the lawn chairs in front of the house I shared with Austin.

They'd turned the lights on early so it was hard to tell when day ended and night began. And even with the brightness I still yawned.

"Tired?" Austin asked.

"Exhausted," I said with a little frown. "I have no idea how I'm going to make it until morning."

"I don't think we have to," Marty said gesturing toward a couple of the houses nearby. Some of the people were making their way inside waving and wishing everyone a good night.

The curtains closed on the nearest house and minutes later the lights inside went out. There was a light on each wall of the outside of the house, but the lights surrounding the property did a sufficient job of lighting the area for miles.

"I don't hear them," I said after a long moment of silence.

"You don't hear what?" Mallory asked.

"The creatures," I said peering out toward the fence. The darkness was probably at least a half a mile away. "I don't see their glowing eyes out there either."

Mallory clapped her hands together softly. "Maybe they really are gone."

"We can only hope," Marty said flicking a look at Mallory. She instantly blushed. Marty stretched his arms over his head and let out a yawn that was entirely fake. "Well, I think it's time to turn in don't you think, Mal?"

"Yeah," she said mimicking his yawn but her grin gave away where her thoughts had gone.

"Eww," I said and she flapped her hand at me. "No, he's my brother, it's totally eww."

Mallory stood next to Marty and wrapped her hands around his arm. Her eyelids rapidly blinking as she looked up into his eyes. "Your handsome brother."

"Our mom always told him that too," I teased.

"Shut up, Lucy," Marty said wrapping his arm around Mallory's shoulders as they slipped inside their small home.

Noah leaned forward in his chair and grunted as he stood. "I'm actually tired. I wish I had someone to take to bed with me but she'd be disappointed because I actually want to sleep."

"Good night, Noah," Austin said as Noah turned and walked into his house. It was only a few seconds before the lights turned off.

"Do you think we're being too trusting?" I asked leaning closer to Austin. A cool breeze picked up and prickled my skin.

Austin shrugged. "Everyone here looks pretty happy."

"They do," I said watching another slightly older couple go into their small house.

The curtain was open at the side of the house and I could see a baby's mobile hanging from the ceiling when they flicked the light on for a moment. Small cries ripped through the air stopping the instant the baby's mom appeared. Seconds later the curtains closed and the light turned off.

"You want one of those one day?" Austin asked.

"One of what?"

"A baby."

My throat dried. "Do you?"

"Yeah, of course." He stood and stuck his hand. "But you didn't answer the question."

I took his hand and stood next to him. "Someday. Yeah. If all of this comes to an end, I could see having one."

"Yeah," Austin said leading me toward the house. "We should probably talk marriage first anyway, right?"

I smiled as he walked into the house. I stopped and looked out into the darkness.

"You coming?" Austin asked.

"Yeah, one second."

I drew in a breath of the chilly air and let it inflate my lungs. It was a cleansing breath. I looked up at the sky and closed my eyes.

There had been a lot of loss. The world around us was completely different and probably wouldn't ever be the same.

I exhaled and turned back toward the house. We could make it a good life again. It would be up to us to rebuild and there wasn't anyone I would have rather been with than Austin. And Marty, Noah, and Mallory.

We were going to be okay. And even though it was going to be hard, we were going to try to find some happiness in what was left.

Marriage?

Babies?

I didn't know about any of that. But the possibilities brought a smile to my face. And knowing that Austin was interested in any of those things warmed my insides.

We had our guardian angels looking over us. They'd get us through whatever was thrown our way.

"Come inside. I'm getting lonely," Austin called. The bedsprings squeaked as he lowered himself down.

I didn't wait. Everything I wanted at that moment, was inside the house. I closed the door and locked it.

BOOKS BY KELLEE L. GREENE

From Below Series

Creatures - Book 1

Desolation - Book 2

Red Sky Series

Red Sky - Book 1

Blue Cloud - Book 2

Black Rain - Book 3

White Dust - Book 4

Indigo Ice - Book 5

Yellow Heat - Book 6

Ravaged Land Series

Ravaged Land -Book 1

Finding Home - Book 2

Crashing Down - Book 3

Running Away - Book 4

Escaping Fear - Book 5

Fighting Back - Book 6

Ravaged Land: Divided Series

The Last Disaster - Book 1

The Last Remnants - Book 2

The Last Struggle - Book 3

Falling Darkness Series

Unholy - Book 1

Uprising - Book 2

Hunted - Book 3

The Island Series

The Island - Book 1

The Fight - Book 2

The Escape - Book 3

The Erased - Book 4

The Alien Invasion Series

The Landing - Book 1

The Aftermath - Book 2

Destined Realms Series

Destined - Book 1

Sign up for Kellee L. Greene's mailing list for new releases, sales, cover reveals and more!

Sign up: http://eepurl.com/bJLmrL

You can Find Kellee on Facebook:

www.facebook.com/kelleelgreene

ABOUT THE AUTHOR

Kellee L. Greene is a stay-at-home-mom to two super awesome and wonderfully sassy children. She loves to read, draw and spend time with her family when she's not writing. Writing and having people read her books has been a long time dream of hers and she's excited to write more. Her favorites genres are Fantasy and Sci-fi. Kellee lives in Wisconsin with her husband, two kids and two cats.

For more information:
www.kelleelgreene.com

facebook.com/kelleelgreene

twitter.com/kelleelgreene

bookbub.com/authors/kellee-l-greene

instagram.com/kelleelgreene